Down the Bright Stream

Dodder, Baldmoney, Cloudberry, and Sneezewort are the last gnomes left in England, and were first introduced to readers in the award-winning book, *The Little Grey Men*.

This book opens with the four gnomes snugly tucked up in their oak tree for the winter—but they are awoken from their sleep with the terrible news that the Folly Brook is drying up and they must move at once. So the four brothers set off in their boat, the *Jeanie Deans*, to find a new home where they will be really safe.

'B.B.' was born as D. J. Watkins-Pitchford in 1905 in Northamptonshire. He studied at the Royal College of Art and was for many years the art master at Rugby School. He has written many books for both children and adults, all of which reflect his naturalist's knowledge and passion for the countryside. *The Little Grey Men* and its sequel, *Down the Bright Stream*, are two of his most well-known and best-loved books and in 1942 *The Little Grey Men* won the prestigious Carnegie Medal.

D1027921

Down the Bright Stream

Other Oxford Books

'B.B.'

Down the Bright Stream

Illustrated by D. J. Watkins-Pitchford ARCA

OXFORD
UNIVERSITY PRESS

OXFORD

UNIVERSITY PRESS

Great Clarendon Street, Oxford OX2 6DP

Oxford University Press is a department of the University of Oxford.
It furthers the University's objective of excellence in research, scholarship,
and education by publishing worldwide in

Oxford New York

Auckland Cape Town Dar es Salaam Hong Kong Karachi
Kuala Lumpur Madrid Melbourne Mexico City Nairobi
New Delhi Shanghai Taipei Toronto

With offices in

Argentina Austria Brazil Chile Czech Republic France Greece
Guatemala Hungary Italy Japan Poland Portugal Singapore
South Korea Switzerland Thailand Turkey Ukraine Vietnam

Oxford is a registered trade mark of Oxford University Press
in the UK and in certain other countries

Database right Oxford University Press (maker)

First published 1948 by Eyre & Spottiswoode
First published by Oxford University Press 2001

8

British Library Cataloguing in Publication Data

ISBN 978-0-19-279204-4

Printed in Great Britain

Paper used in the production of this book is a natural,
recyclable product made from wood grown in sustainable forests.
The manufacturing process conforms to the environmental
regulations of the country of origin.

For my daughter
Angela June

Contents

The wonder of the world, the beauty and the power, the shapes of things, their colours, lights, and shades; these I saw. Look ye also while life lasts.

CHAPTER ONE

A Rude Awakening

 f you have read *The Little Grey Men* you will know all about the Oak Tree House and the Stream People, and how three gnomes—Dodder (a lame gnome), Baldmoney, and Sneezewort—went up the Folly Brook to look for their lost brother Cloudberry, and how they discovered him, after many adventures, fit and well and full of high spirits.

You will remember too all about the *Jeanie Deans*, a toy ship they found on Poplar Island, what fun they had aboard her and how they all went back to Oak Tree House on the banks of a Warwickshire brook.

If you have not read it, it doesn't matter; perhaps you will one day before very long.

These four—Dodder, Baldmoney, Sneezewort, and Cloudberry—were the last gnomes left in England. All the others, and the fairies who used to inhabit the green places and the streams, had long ago disappeared but our gnomes had survived for so long because they lived in a very secure and ancient Oak Tree in a remote part of the Warwickshire countryside. They had managed to avoid coming into contact with the Mortals for hundreds of years, and, believe me, *that* took a bit of doing! For this very same reason the badger survives to this day: one of the oldest animals we have, he has endured simply because he never shows himself during the day (except when he is ill or old) and is very particular *never* to get mixed up with Mortals and their quarrels and he never (or very rarely) steals their property, as is the habit of the foxes, rats, and some wild birds.

Soon after the gnomes got back to Oak Tree House after their hair-raising adventures, I left the district where they lived. I often wondered what happened to them because I knew that men were at work spoiling the Folly Brook and all the lovely country in those parts. And perhaps I never should have known their fate if it were not for a little bird, who told me the rest of their adventures. From what he narrated to me I have managed to piece together the following book. It happened this way.

One April morning quite recently, when I was in Pricket Wood watching a Bottle-tit[1] build its nest, a tiny yellow bird came hopping about among the blackthorn just over my head and I recognized Peewee, the Willow Wren, newly arrived from Africa.

[1] Long-tailed Tit

It was Peewee who gave me the facts. He had them from his wife's cousin who happened to live by the Folly Brook, so you may be sure he was telling the truth and Woodcock had also told him a great deal. But Peewee was a bad story-teller and he had to stop every now and then to look for caterpillars and other little green insects, besides which he was still very tired after his long journey. So I will tell you myself in my own way, just as I did in the first book.

Well, after the Animal Banquet (that is a sort of jolly feast) in Oak Tree House, and all the birds and beasts went home, the gnomes and Squirrel fell fast to sleep. The fire went out and it became very cold inside the tree. But the gnomes were as warm as a litter of puppies. They all squeezed up, one against the other, and tucked the dead bracken bed around them and then they snored and snored. December passed, January came, (what a bitter winter that was too!) with the snow piling up in drifts about the oak tree root and the Folly was like black iron. It was a bad time for the Stream People. February came and still the snow lay. Sometimes it thawed and became all dirty and brown, but soon fresh snow would come and whiten it again.

It was not until mid-March that one could feel the spring stirring. At last the Folly brook was unbound and could sing its old sweet song, buds appeared on the willow trees and the Tits, Blue Button, Bottle Button (the Long-Tailed tit), Black Bonnet (the Marsh tit), and Spink the chaffinch, began to get busy in the hedges and woods. The watervoles came out of their holes and sat in the sun, warming themselves, and the red-gartered moorhens began to think about nest building.

Big winds came roaring over the greening water meadows, weeding out every rotten tree and pulling them out of the ground. The March wind is Nature's dentist, it pulls out every decayed stump and rotten branch and makes the trees sound and well again.

And how busy the peewits were over the ploughlands, tumbling about in the pale windy sunlight crying 'A week, a week, two bullocks a week!' It was good to think the bitter winter had passed.

And then, one such windy day, when the Folly flashed and the first celandines gleamed on the warm bank, newly painted with yellow varnish, there came a scrabbling on the door of Oak Tree House. 'Scratch! Scratch! Scratch!'

Dodder was the first to stir. And how stiff he was! He pushed away the bracken and stuck his big nose out like a sleepy dormouse.

Sure enough, someone was scratching very loudly on their front door! Now this was a great breach of animal etiquette. Never before had the Stream People dared to disturb them from their winter sleep. Dodder was so puzzled and annoyed he awoke the others.

'Hi! Baldmoney. Ho! Cloudberry! Hey! Sneezewort! Wake up! Wake up! There's someone scratching on the door!'

Baldmoney turned over with a grunt and sat up, his beard full of bracken bits. 'Someone at the door?'

'Yes, listen!'

Scratch, scratch, scratch.

'Disgustin'. What are the Stream People thinkin' of?'

'Go and see who it is,' commanded Dodder, rummaging about among the bracken for his leg. 'Tell 'em to go away, give 'em a piece of your mind.'

Baldmoney grunted. Particles of bracken had got down his neck and he felt all tickly and irritable.

He felt his way to the door and undid the bolts and bars. When he opened it, the flood of brilliant light and rush of cold sweet air blinded him. He passed his hand over his face and then he sneezed so violently he fell over.

'Who's there? What do you want?'

'It's me, Watervole,' came a squeaky voice. 'We thought you ought to wake up because something dreadful's happening.'

Baldmoney opened his left eye a tiny way and slowly he became used to the blaze of light.

Soon he could make out the familiar form of Watervole appearing extremely agitated.

The poor animal was so upset he could hardly speak or make himself clear. 'Oh dear, it's awful, it's *awful!*'

'What's awful?' asked Baldmoney irritably, for he was not yet quite awake.

'Why, the Folly—it's getting so low and we don't know what's the matter. All our galleries and holes are high and dry and there's only just a trickle of water coming down!'

'Well, I expect it's because of the dry weather,' said Baldmoney, rubbing his eyes. 'Don't get so flustered, Watervole, it isn't like you.'

'But there's been plenty of rain, it can't be that. We're afraid the Miller's been playing some tricks up at Moss Mill and he's stopped the water. All the Stream People are worried about it. Some of the voles from Lucking's meadows are moving house because they think there'll be more water down this way.'

By now Baldmoney's eyes had become accustomed

to the light. He stood there with bracken and dried grass in his beard and gazed at the Folly. And I must say he had a nasty shock. On the oak root was a pale bleached band quite a foot in width which showed the usual height of the water. Normally they could almost launch their fishing boats from the very doorstep of Oak Tree House but now the level was far below and in place of the brown pool there was a wide expanse of wet green shingle.

'All right, Watervole, I'll fetch the others. Dodder'll be here in a minute.'

'What's the trouble?' Dodder was at his elbow. He had put on his bone leg and like Baldmoney was rubbing his eyes in the unaccustomed glare of day.

'The Folly—look at it!' exclaimed Baldmoney, now thoroughly alarmed. 'Looks as if it was running dry or something.'

By now Sneezewort and Cloudberry had appeared and Squirrel too. They all staggered sleepily down the wet shingle to have a look.

'This is serious,' said Dodder. 'Looks as if we're all going to be left high and dry, and see who's coming down the stream!'

Round the bend above the Oak Tree came a party of water voles and seven or eight distracted moorhens. 'Looks as if they were in a hurry, let's ask them what's the matter.'

In a few moments the frightened birds and animals came up to them. 'It's awful,' gasped a mother vole. 'The stream isn't running at all now up by Lucking's meadows, only the pools hold water and the *fish!*—you should see them kicking about on the shingle!'

Dodder, who had been looking at the stream with a keen eye suddenly gasped, 'Pan save us! Look at the fish in the pool—they're all going downstream.'

The others followed his gaze and, sure enough, it was as Dodder had said. The amber depths were alive with fleeing fish. They were passing in cloudy shadows, hundreds and hundreds of fish: perch, roach, and minnows, all jostling each other, pushing and darting, with fear writ large in their jewelled eyes.

'That's bad,' said Dodder. 'They know something's up too.'

One of the watervoles began to snivel. 'What's to become of us all if the Folly dries up?' she wailed. 'Where shall we go?'

'It's a nice how d'you do I must say,' said Dodder gruffly. 'Just when we're still half-awake like this and all set for the summer fishing. But it's no good panicking . . . Hullo, here comes the King of Fishers, *now* we shall know something!'

The kingfisher came direct like a big brilliant blue bee up to his favourite perch on the oak and all the animals crowded round.

But he took no notice of them at first. He puffed himself out and wriggled his throat.

'Hey! King of Fishers,' called Dodder, 'what's up?'

But truth to say, the Kingfisher was so crammed with fish he couldn't get a word out.

'Disgustin',' growled Dodder. 'Perfectly *disgustin'*. Look, he's eaten so much he's nearly bursting!'

If the bird had not been sitting out of reach, I believe Dodder would have shaken him.

'It's no good,' piped up Sneezewort. 'We shall have to wait now till he's digested his meal.'

The Kingfisher seemed to be trying to say something. He made several attempts but no sound would come and after a minute the gorged bird relaxed into a stupor. Baldmoney, shaking with rage, picked up a pebble and threw it up with deadly accuracy. It struck the Kingfisher on the beak and it so surprised him he immediately coughed up five sticklebacks, which fell on the shingle at Dodder's feet. One hit Watervole on the nose, which made everybody laugh.

'*Now* perhaps you'll tell, King of Fishers,' said Dodder icily.

'Marvellous!' said the Kingfisher dreamily. 'Never had such fishing in all my life! Why, every pool and stickle is simply *stiff* with fish. Glorious!' he exclaimed again. 'Wonderful!'

'Never mind about the *fishing*,' shouted Dodder, almost beside himself with rage. He had quite forgotten to treat the Kingfisher with respect; there was no time for ceremony. 'Tell us what's the trouble, why is the Folly drying up?'

All the answer they got, however, was a splash. Kingfisher had dived straight down over their heads into the pool. He emerged a second later with a minnow in his beak, which he carried up to the oak twig and beat insensible before turning it round and gulping it down.

'Marvellous fishin',' said the Kingfisher again, in a dreamy sort of way.

Dodder was now so incensed he could hardly contain himself. He turned to Squirrel. 'Can't you *do* something, Squirrel. Climb up the tree and shake some sense into him?'

'All right, gnomes,' said the Kingfisher, as Squirrel began to advance towards the oak. 'I can't tell you much. All I know is the water's dropping and the fish . . . '

'Never mind the fish,' interrupted Dodder, 'can't you go up to Moss Mill and find out what's happening?'

'Oh well, I'll do that, Dodder, if you want me to, but personally I don't see why you're all getting so excited.'

'Well, anything might have happened,' said Squirrel indignantly. 'The miller must have done something.'

'All right, I'll go,' replied the Kingfisher. 'One more minnow first though, watch me catch this one!'

Down he went again into the pool, sending the spray right and left. The others could only sigh and sadly shake their heads at one another.

When the greedy bird had eaten this last fish he darted off away up the Folly. They watched the speck of vivid blue speeding round the bend until it was lost to sight. After the maddening bird had departed, Baldmoney went under the bank and cut a willow stick. This he pushed into the sand just on the edge of the water and made a little notch with his hunting knife where the ripples wetted the wand. Then everyone sat down on the stones and watched it. The level of the stream must have been falling very slowly because at first there was no noticeable drop. But after a quarter of an hour had passed the notch was the minutest fraction above the water. Yes, there was no doubt about it, the Folly *was* getting lower, very soon it would be dry!

Cannot you picture the pathetic plight of all those little people gathered there upon the sandy shores of the oak tree pool? The sun was shining so brightly, the water meadows were such a vivid green and a gentle breeze was silvering the slender willow thickets. Overhead white clouds, like soft pillows, were drifting slowly before the west wind, blackbirds and thrushes were singing, and away over Collinson Church a kestrel hovered just like a small red paper kite.

It was a shame that such a bright spring morning should be so heavy with impending disaster. For the Folly meant everything to the gnomes. It had been their loved companion for generations, it had provided them with fish, it had sung them to sleep, it had borne them safely back from the perils of Poplar Island and sinister Crow Wood. It was quite unthinkable that this bright and happy stream should ever go.

With horror-stricken eyes they gazed at the willow stick, hoping against hope that their fears were groundless. The only one who appeared unconcerned was Cloudberry.

He swaggered up and down the beach with his thumbs stuck in his belt whistling through his teeth. The truth was, that ever since he had been to Spitzbergen with the wild geese, he thought himself no end of a gnome and the possibility of leaving the Oak Tree and the Folly didn't worry him a bit.

'I wish you'd stop whistling, Cloudberry,' said Dodder irritably. 'Come and see if you think the water's dropped any more.'

'Pooh! Why worry anyway? If we've got to move downstream, who cares? Who wants to stay in the same place all their lives, anyway? *I* like seeing new country. If only I had wings like the King of Fishers! That's a fine bird for you, *he's* the one to get about! The beastly old Folly can go on dropping for all I care, I'm all for the open road and high adventure. What's the good of looking like a lot of gravedigger beetles? Anyone might think that the end of the world had come,' and he turned a somersault on the shingle.

Dodder did not deign to reply. He got up and hobbled along to where they had moored the *Jeanie Deans*.

Alas! she was no longer the bright spick-and-span ship they had left tied up under the bank that snowy night four months before.

She lay half on her side in the shallow water, red rust covered her keel and green slime draped her stern. Even her name, *Jeanie Deans*, had been half-washed out by the rigorous winter weather. Baldmoney and Sneezewort scrambled up on to her sloping decks. Rainwater had collected in the hold and several snails had taken up their abode in the wheelhouse. Baldmoney indignantly wrenched them off and threw them onto the bank, where a big spotted thrush speedily pounced upon them and carried them off. Song thrushes love snails, they prefer them to worms. He took them one by one and smashed them on a large white stone by the stream side and then came back and begged for more, but he never offered to help. Meanwhile Baldmoney was rummaging about in the cabin. Old oak leaves had half-filled it, the whole place smelt damp and musty and the bunks were full of wood-lice.

'Disgustin' mess,' muttered Baldmoney as he looked about him. 'It'll need a whole day to spring-clean her.'

'Let's start in on her now,' said Sneezewort. 'We won't ask Cloudberry, he won't help. I'll bet he thinks she's a rotten old hulk anyway.'

He kicked a lot of leaves into a corner and gathered them up in his arms. Baldmoney climbed down the side and went back to the oak for the frog-skin bucket and a scrubbing brush.

Gnomes are cleanly little folk and the sight of their lovely ship in such a state was a grievous thing.

Very soon that tiny strip of wet sand behind the oak tree presented a very busy scene indeed. There's nothing like a job on hand for banishing depression and worry. The *Jeanie Deans* had to be spring-cleaned anyway, whether she would be wanted at once or next week, and at last even Cloudberry condescended to lend a hand. Back came Baldmoney with the bucket of water and a scrubbing brush. The latter was not of his own making.

It may amuse you to know that it was really the head of a toothbrush and had once belonged to none other than the miller at Moss Mill! He had bought it three years before in the local Woolworth's and it had seen good service. When the bristles began to come out the miller used it for cleaning the spokes and hubs of a new bicycle which he was very proud of. He had a puppy and one day the puppy stole the toothbrush and took it down to the riverside to play with it. It fell over the mill dam and the puppy watched it splash into the water with his little head cocked right on one side. The current bore it to the tail of the pool and there it lay among the rushes for some time until the winter floods rolled it on down. Baldmoney had found it under a willow root close to Joppa. That was the history of the scrubbing brush, though of course the gnomes knew nothing of its story nor why the Mortals used such a brush.

Dodder called the poor anxious voles and waterhens together and told them not to worry but to come and help spring-clean the *Jeanie Deans*. Soon some Bub'ms (rabbits) joined them and a tit or two, and Squirrel. The latter being most agile and strong, made himself very useful.

They fetched a ladder from the stores in the Oak Tree so that Dodder could climb aboard and the voles could get up and down without any difficulty. Many beaks and paws make light work and in a very short while the *Jeanie Deans* was looking quite smart again. They worked so hard they forgot all about the Folly and the voles forgot about ruined homes and their neatly tunnelled galleries which were now high and dry. Nobody heeded the constant procession of fish which were passing endlessly downstream; they even forgot the King of Fishers. Baldmoney went on all fours and scrubbed like any old seasoned charwoman until his little face was the colour of a bilberry. Sneezewort scraped off all the red rust from the hull. Cloudberry went to and fro with an empty snail shell, baling out all the water which had collected in the hold and once, just out of spite, he emptied the contents down Sneezewort's neck, and the latter squeaked indignantly like a mouse. The watervoles got busy on the green slime, gnawing it off with their sharp teeth, and the tits flew in and out of the cabin with dead leaves in their bills.

In the middle of all this bustle and activity the King of Fishers miraculously appeared on the oak branch above. For a moment or two he surveyed the scene without speaking. Nobody noticed him sitting there.

Then he whistled once, loud and long, and instantly everyone stopped work.

They crowded round the shingle underneath him; nobody said a word.

Then the Kingfisher spoke. 'Well, Stream People, I've got bad news for you. I've been up above the Mill and you wouldn't recognize the place. There's a whole gang of men, clearing the Folly Brook and digging an underground drain. There isn't a bush or a tree along the banks all the way to Crow Wood. They are taking the water right under the hill to the new reservoir beyond Collinson. *That's* where our Folly's going. In another week there won't be enough water in the brook to float a fiddler (a fiddler is a water skater), so it looks as if we shall *all* have to make a move. The bank where my wife and I have built our nest for generations just isn't there!'

'We are all in the same boat then,' said Dodder, after a horrified gasp had gone up from everyone. 'You'll have to move too.'

Baldmoney, who had said no word, put down his frog-skin bucket and mopped his forehead. 'You've said it, Dodder, we're all in the same boat and that boat is the *Jeanie Deans*! In another day there won't be enough water to float her at the rate the stream's dropping. We must all get away tonight!'

'Come on!' shouted Dodder, suddenly galvanized to life. 'All hands to work on the *Jeanie Deans*! Squirrel, you and Sneezewort start getting the stores on board. Baldmoney and I will get the contents of the cellar down to the hold. I'm not going to leave all that wine to go to waste, every scrap of food must be under hatches by sunset! And you voles and moorhens had better lend a hand too, if you've the time to spare.'

'I'll be getting downstream to tell my wife and the rest of the Stream People,' exclaimed the Kingfisher, who was now very sobered at what he had seen and a little ashamed of himself too for his earlier boorish behaviour.

'Good luck to your Majesty,' said Dodder, polite for the first time that day, 'and thank you for helping us.'

After the King of Fishers had gone everybody set to with a will. They put out two more gangplanks from the shingle to the hull and there was a constant procession of animals and gnomes up and down it. Some carried leaf sacks of acorn bread and wheaten ears, others bundles of dried sticklebacks; Squirrel carried little bags of nuts (popping a nut into his mouth on the sly).

Reverently the snail shells, sealed, and full of Dodder's precious vintage berry wines, were laid all a-row on the shingle. Dodder would not let anyone save himself carry them aboard for fear they would be shaken up. He held the shells in a certain way, for he was an experienced connoisseur of wine.

By nightfall all stores were safely under hatches. It only now remained to get the ship down the bank and into the stream.

Already Baldmoney's tell-tale stick was high and dry, the Folly had dropped a foot since morning. There was not a moment to lose!

CHAPTER TWO

The Exodus

nomes as well as mortals must have sleep. I have told in the first book how they prefer going about their business at night, for the very good reason that during daylight they might be seen. This especially applies to the early part of the year when there are few leaves on the bushes and the grass, flowers, and weeds have not begun to grow.

You must remember that it was yet early spring and the Little Men would normally have only just begun to think about stirring.

They had been aroused from their deep hibernation a week too soon and they had hardly time to collect their wits. This dreadful calamity was so sudden and upsetting. Without warning they found themselves faced with a complete uprooting of their home, where they had dwelt for nearly five hundred years, and all because a few miles away some men had been told to dig a new bed for the Folly!

It was indeed lucky for the gnomes that the weather was kind. It was early March and had there been snow on the ground and hard frost I really cannot say *what* would have happened to Dodder and his brothers. Perhaps they would have perished like all the other gnomes who used to live among the fields and forests of medieval Britain.

The Little Men had been working all day loading the *Jeanie Deans* and they were tired out. When darkness fell the voles and other Stream People went away downstream and the gnomes were left alone. They decided that they must have a short sleep before trying to launch the ship and Dodder asked Ben the owl, who lived up in the oak, to wake them before midnight, otherwise they might have overslept. I forgot to mention that Ben had been terribly upset when he had heard the news. But he said he was going to stay on in the oak tree whatever happened. He and his forebears had lived there since the oak tree was three hundred years old and he did not depend on the Folly for a living. It is true he liked the stream, indeed he had once said that he would never live out of the sound of water, but he had talked the whole thing over with his wife and they had decided to stay.

The four weary little creatures, and Squirrel too, huddled up inside the tree for their last nap in the old home.

They were too upset to talk very much. Sneezewort of course snuffled a good deal, but the others managed to control their feelings and Cloudberry, as I said before, seemed to treat the whole affair as rather a joke.

He kept on saying 'Of course we (meaning the wild geese and himself) WE would think nothing of this out in Spitzbergen,' and then he began a long story of how once an Arctic fox stole all the eggs out of a goose's nest and the mother goose had to find another site and how he helped her. Dodder soon shut him up.

They scraped together the dead bracken to make a bed and in a few moments everybody was asleep and had forgotten all about the happenings of the last few hours. When at last Ben's voice came hooting down inside the hollow oak they awoke quite fresh and ready.

'Don't worry, gnomes,' said old Ben kindly. 'I'll bet you three fat field mice that you'll come back one day and we shall all meet again in this old tree, and that the Folly will come to life again.'

'I hope you're right,' faltered Dodder, trying very hard to keep a tremor from his voice. 'It's awful leaving the old place, and you too, Ben. You've been a true friend to us, we can't ever repay you. You've found us skins for our clothes and done us many a good turn one way and another.'

'Oh, I've done nothing,' said Ben gruffly, and there was a shake in his voice too, 'I shall miss you no end in the old tree, even though you did smoke me out sometimes! And here's a little present, Dodder, for all of you. My wife and I couldn't let you go without something to remember us by.' From the darkness above four lovely velvety moleskins dropped down and fell at Dodder's feet. 'They'll keep out the cold,' added Ben, more gruffly still, and he turned abruptly and vanished back into his nesting hole above.

Dodder and his brothers took up the skins. They were beauties and would make them grand coats which would last for years. 'Well, that's very nice of you, Ben,' Dodder called out. 'They certainly will remind us of you, every time we wear them.'

I must here break in on this touching scene with a piece of information. As the gnomes never killed warm-blooded animals, for the voles, mice, birds, and four-footed beasts—with the sole exception of wood dogs (foxes) and stoats—were their very good friends. But skins were the best possible clothing and there's nothing like moleskin for keeping a gnome nice and warm. Every time they came across a mouse or mole and saw him looking suspiciously at their coats they had to explain how they had come by them. Now, without Ben as a fur trapper, what would they do? One consolation was that these fine new skins which Ben had given them would last for a very long time. Their old mouse and mole skins had seen good service and were wearing very thin.

With one last look round the oak root they trooped down the shingle to the *Jeanie Deans*.

She was now about two feet from the water but the sand and shingle sloped fairly steeply and with Squirrel's help they soon pushed her down. She went into the stream stern first in the approved style and in a moment or two all were aboard.

'Goodbye, Ben!' they shouted, as the ship began to feel the current. 'GOOOOD BOOOOO!' quavered Ben and there was a very pronounced shake in his voice. 'GOOOOD BOOOOO! GOO GOOO BOOOOO!'

As they slowly drifted away down the dark stream they heard Ben's voice growing fainter and fainter until it died away. Dodder sighed. 'He was a grand old chap was Ben.'

'He was indeed,' replied Baldmoney. 'As fine a bird as ever gulped a mouse.'

'Ben was a good sort, I don't deny,' said Cloudberry, 'but I don't think you can compare a bird like that to a—'

'*I* know, a *wild goose!*' burst out Dodder. 'I *do* wish you'd shut up about the Heaven Hounds. Old Ben had a heart of gold.'

'Can't see why he wanted to stick in one place though,' said Cloudberry. 'You should see the Snowy owls now, they're twice the size of Ben, and as white as snow. I once—'

'Oh! shut up, Cloudberry!' snapped Dodder again. 'I'm just about sick of hearing about all your wonderful doings. Go below and help Sneezewort with the supper, I'm starving.'

Cloudberry moved sulkily away, muttering to himself, and Dodder stared into the darkness.

The great masses of the elms and pollarded willows, the dense thorn bushes on the banks loomed darkly over them. Even though they were as yet bare of leaves they seemed vast and heavy in the dim light.

Dodder sighed deeply. There was no elation in his breast such as when they were last aboard the *Jeanie Deans*. And then he had a curious feeling that, after all, this ghastly happening was all for the best, that it had all been planned. Supposing they had not gone up the Folly last year to hunt for Cloudberry, why, they would never have found the *Jeanie Deans*! And if they hadn't got the *Jeanie Deans*, even though her engines were useless, what would have become of them? They would have had to set out on foot, and at this time of year the dangers would have been great. At any time the weather might turn cold and there was no cover along the banks. Perhaps Pan was still watching over them, perhaps he had sent them the boat for this very purpose. Dodder sighed again.

He leant his arms on the rail in front of him and stared at the stars. What a beautiful calm night it was! Scarce a cloud to be seen and a sickle moon hung among the fretted willow wands which glided so softly past.

He heard the very low and secret chuckle of the dying Folly as it swirled around some projecting root. Where would they be by morning? They would have to tie up somewhere, of course. Would the water still be deep enough to float them? Already the current had borne them beyond familiar places. Dodder noted trees and bushes he had never seen before. The Folly took unfamiliar turns and twists. He hoped there were no waterfalls or weirs.

Now and again he heard the plop of a water vole and once he saw three of them swimming alongside. They, like themselves, were refugees. Dodder called softly into the darkness and asked them if they were making downstream. But the voles only shook their muzzles and went on swimming.

The *Jeanie Deans* was slowly turning round and round as she drifted in the current. Had they the engines going this would not have happened, but without power she was at the mercy of the stream. Now and again she bumped gently against some protruding branch or sunken snag, once she stuck for a moment on a mass of floating reed, but the current of the Folly had her in safe keeping and wheeled her out and on.

With one last look at the stars Dodder turned and went below. He found a cosy sight there. Sneezewort had lit the little lamp over the cabin table and had drawn the curtains. Supper was laid, nuts for Squirrel, and fried mushroom and fish for themselves. As a great treat Dodder produced a snail-shell full of blackberry wine, some of his best.

It was surprising how much better they felt when the meal was done. Dodder made up his mind he would not worry any more, they were in Pan's keeping, they must trust in him.

They crawled into the little bunks and tucked themselves in and soon all but Dodder were asleep. He lay long awake. Not worrying; oh dear no, his mind was at peace now, a curious comfortable peace enveloped him. He felt the gentle movement of the boat and heard now and again the faint sound of weeds brushing the hull and the chuckle and gurgle of the stream bearing them on. Why worry? What was the use? Something shook the bunk opposite. It was Squirrel scratching. Perhaps he had caught a flea. Good old Squirrel! It was cosy having him with them. I think it shows to what desperate straits the gnomes had been driven, to abandon themselves to the mercy of the stream in this way, without even keeping a watch on board. It was all very well to trust to Pan, but Pan only helps those animals who help themselves.

So all through that long night the Folly bore them on. The *Jeanie Deans* swung and gyrated solemnly in the current. Many times she was swept into a miniature whirlpool and there she stayed, circling for several minutes. And all the time the level was dropping and dropping. Once the foremast caught against a fallen branch and there the ship stuck fast, with a dangerous list. Still the occupants of the cabin slept peacefully on.

Whether or not it was the finger of Pan which lifted that twig and let the ship drift free, or whether it was the drop of the water level, I do not know, but at last the *Jeanie Deans* got clear once more and floated gently on, on an even keel.

The light in the cabin went out (the gnomes used nut oil for burning) and the little lantern, smoking and smelling abominably, swung faintly creaking to and fro in the darkened cabin. Now and again a slight jar passed through the ship, but the mariners never woke.

CHAPTER THREE

The Death of the Folly

odder opened his eyes slowly. His brain was fogged with dreams, strange disturbing dreams, in which their Oak Tree house had been uprooted by a violent gale, leaving them as naked and defenceless as beetles disturbed from under a stone.

What had happened? Where was he? He stared around him at the cabin. A faint light, coming down the companion-way, shone on the pictures on the walls opposite. Slowly the events of the preceding day and night came back to him. Of course! this was the cabin of the *Jeanie Deans*, they were refugees without a home now that the old oak tree was no longer able to shelter and protect them.

How far had they drifted since last night? Dodder sat

up suddenly and rubbed his eyes. The others were sleeping soundly. He could see no visible trace of them under the skin rugs in the opposite bunk and only the fluffy tip of Squirrel's tail protruded from his blanket.

There was no motion in the ship, no sense of movement. Quickly he pulled aside one of the little curtains and looked out. His heart sank. They were aground! Opposite was a red bank of earth drilled with old sand-martins' holes. Three small ash trees grew precariously on that steep little cliff.

A swift run of muddy water still flowed a few yards away but he could see shingle and sand just below the porthole and, even as he looked, the *Jeanie Deans* gave a sickening lurch to starboard and all the plates and crockery slid off the cabin table onto the floor with a loud crash.

The noise awoke the others. Baldmoney jumped from his bunk wild-eyed, his hand on his knife. Cloudberry and Sneezewort were tipped right out of their bunks under the cabin table where they rolled among the plates and bedding.

Squirrel managed somehow to hold on to the side of his bunk and with one spring he was out of the cabin door. Dodder had been prepared for the worst. His hand clutched the edge of his bunk and he just saved himself.

'Wha-what's up?' stuttered Sneezewort, his eyes big with fear.

'Aground I guess,' said Dodder. 'Hard and fast too. Let's get up on deck.'

Picking their way along the sloping floor they joined Squirrel on the tilted bridge.

Dodder was right. Aground they were, 'good and proper', right in mid-stream too and in full view of either bank. Moreover, day was breaking and it was bitterly cold. The *Jeanie Deans* had gone aground on a shingle bed, right in the centre of the stream. At normal water level the ship would have passed over with inches to spare but with the falling stream she had not had a chance. One thing was in their favour, they were still among meadows, and bushes and trees grew plentifully along either bank.

Downstream, beyond the tail of the shingle bed, he could see a good deal of water. If only they could get the *Jeanie Deans* over the obstruction they might at least gain the deeper stream and float on to some safe hiding place.

As they stood all together there they spied several water voles with bundles on their backs, coming down-stream. They appeared in a fearful hurry and were strangers, obviously refugees from the upper waters. When they saw the stranded steamer they took to the banks and scurried by, despite the fact that Dodder called to them in their own language.

Only the last vole lingered a moment and pointed with his paw upstream and then, without saying a word, he hurried after his companions.

Squirrel hopped over the side, and though he didn't like getting his fur wet, he tried to move the boat. But the task was beyond him.

Baldmoney and Cloudberry waded ashore (the Folly barely came to their knees) and went on down to spy out what lay below.

Dodder and Sneezewort remained on the bridge, shivering with cold and blowing on their fingernails.

'We haven't a chance to get her off unless a miracle happens,' said Dodder. 'She's hard and fast. If we stay here all day somebody will spy us. Our best plan is to leave her and go into hiding close by and try to get her off tonight.'

'The water will be lower then,' said Sneezewort, 'it's running away so fast. There won't be a drop by tonight. I don't see we can do much.'

'Then we shall have to go on foot,' said Dodder grimly, 'and leave the bulk of our supplies aboard. It's a pity, but there it is.'

Not a bird nor a beast was visible. The stream seemed quite deserted. Baldmoney and Cloudberry had passed out of sight round a bend of the bank. Three feet away two minnows were flapping and slapping in a little hollow in the shingle where they had been stranded and in another little pool Sneezewort spied quite twenty little fish frantically trying to wriggle free.

'There's our breakfast at any rate,' said Dodder as he let himself over the side by the rope ladder. 'We might as well have fresh fish for breakfast. We'll get 'em cooked before the others come back.'

It was the work of a moment to capture the unfortunate minnows and they were borne in triumph back to the ship. Sneezewort speedily got the stove going and by the time Baldmoney and the others returned they found a nice hot breakfast awaiting them.

And they brought a ray of hope with them. Not more than a hundred yards below, the Folly joined a big stream. Indeed, it was more than a stream, Baldmoney said, it was a river, a real wide river, three times the size of the Folly.

'If only we had got through we should have been safe,' said Baldmoney. 'Can't we try and push her along over the shingle?' But Squirrel shook his head. 'Not a hope,' he said. 'Even if we all pushed her we couldn't move her.'

'Well, it's no good worrying,' said Dodder. 'Let's have some breakfast and then talk things over. It's pretty early yet by the sun and we may hit on a plan.'

So they set to with a will and very soon all those minnows had disappeared and Squirrel, who was not very fond of fish, disposed of a surprising quantity of nuts.

Just as they were finishing their meal there came a sudden rapping on the hull and Dodder, peering nervously through a porthole, uttered a shout of delight, for he saw the friendly squat head of an otter.

In no time everyone was out of the cabin and up on deck. To their delight they found it was a relation of their old friend Otter, who met such a sad end in Crow Wood at the hands of cruel Giant Grum. He was a sleek well-grown beast but he looked very worried. 'I'm off downstream, gnomes,' he said. 'I saw this ship aground and thought I'd knock and see if there was anyone at home.'

'Well, you couldn't have come at a better moment!' exclaimed Dodder. 'We're in a bad fix. The ship's firmly aground and we can't get her off. We had to leave Oak Tree House last night because the Folly was dropping so quickly. Where have you come from, Otter?'

'All the way from Joppa,' replied the otter, 'and it's a good thing you *did* leave last night. Your Oak Tree Pool hasn't enough water in it to cover a minnow now and every rapid is bone dry. You only just made it. As for my holt under the willow, that's dry too, that's why I'm coming downstream. If I were you I shouldn't waste a moment here, gnomes. Let's try and get the ship off. There's a big river lower down; if you can reach that you will be safe.'

So the gnomes and Squirrel scrambled out of the cabin

and down the rope ladder on to the shingle. Dodder, who remained in the bows, threw them a rope which Otter took in his teeth. The others formed up behind the ship and at a word from Dodder the struggle began.

It was rough treatment for the *Jeanie Deans*. She was dragged bodily over the shingle, half lying on her side and the alarming crashes and tinkles from the cabin seemed to suggest that their crockery was suffering yet again.

What a business that was! Otter pulled with all his might and main, the gnomes and Squirrel shoved and shoved, digging their feet into the loose gravel, slipping and gasping. Otter was a powerful beast and his weight told. The heavy little ship jerked slowly forward, ploughing quite a furrow in the sand and stones as she went, and at last the water lapped her keel. With a final squirm of his powerful rudder, Otter pulled her down into the stream and very soon all were aboard, puffing and gasping and quite out of breath.

Dodder was delighted. He waved his cap gaily to Otter who, now his job was done, began to go on downstream. It did not take long to reach the main river which Baldmoney had told the others about.

The Folly took a sharp bend to the right and there was their salvation: a deep, dark river, lined with sedge clumps and willow stumps, with a depth of water enough to float a ship many times the tonnage of the *Jeanie Deans*.

Not far distant was an immense willow tree whose roots formed a natural cave and thither the gnomes guided the ship—no easy matter without her engine. Squirrel and Baldmoney paddled with long sticks and by skilful seamanship and by making use of the slow current they at last edged her right under the root and made her fast.

'Phew!' gasped Dodder when this was done. 'If Otter hadn't come along we should never have got her off. And now,' said he, 'after all our work you must be thirsty. What about broaching a shell-full of Elderberry 1905?' This proposition was hailed with enthusiasm. They all trooped below and Dodder set to work to remove the wooden bung from one of the snail shells.

'Here's to Otter,' he said, raising the shell to his mouth, and one by one they drank the toast, passing the shell from hand to hand. After a rest and a smoke Dodder set everyone to work to clear up the mess.

The rough treatment the *Jeanie Deans* had received on the shingle bank had thrown the cabin into indescribable confusion. Two of their little china plates were shattered beyond repair and things were lying all over the floor. By some lucky chance the pictures had not been broken but their copper stewpan was dented and this would give Baldmoney some trouble to repair. But on the whole, things had gone well. They had won through to this new river, they had found a secure hiding-place, however temporary, and they had at least time to breathe.

When the *Jeanie Deans* was shipshape once again and everyone felt rested, the gnomes and Squirrel got out the dinghy and rowed up to the Folly, or what was left of it.

It was pretty plain that, had they been delayed much longer, their position would indeed have been desperate. They beached the dinghy and with Dodder in the lead they walked almost to the shingle bank which had so nearly spelt disaster.

It was a calm warm evening. To the westwards the sun was down and already the shadows had begun to gather. Not an animal was seen, all the refugees had gone on down, the Great Trek from the upper waters of the Folly was over. Dodder hobbled across to the edge of the wet shingle. He stood for some time rapt in deep thought looking at the wet Folly bed, where water-snails and minnows were vainly trying to find some cover in the last drop of precious moisture.

Then he turned to the others and his seamed little face was strained with sorrow. 'Gnomes,' said he, 'we have come at the right moment, we are witnessing the passing of our beloved stream. For a thousand, thousand years it has flowed for us, a thousand thousand cuckoo years. It will flow no more!'

And all the gnomes, even Cloudberry, bowed their heads and tears dimmed their eyes. As they stood there in the gathering dusk, looking at that last dying trickle, two dark silent forms swung into view upstream. Like monstrous moths they came and lit in the branches of a shattered elm above them. It was Ben and his wife.

'So it has come at last,' said Ben in his deep voice, 'the prophecy of the Stream People has come to pass!'

Dodder looked up quickly, the tears still running into his beard. 'Why, it's Ben and Mrs Ben! We thought you had decided never to leave the Oak Tree!'

'It has come to pass,' said Ben again, regarding the gnomes with solemn eyes, 'the prophecy of the Stream People.'

'And what was that?' asked Dodder in a voice so low that none but the owl's sharp ears could hear him.

'It was said,' went on the owl, 'that when the Folly ceased to run the Little Grey Men would go and leave the stream for ever!'

'But why,' said Dodder at last, when he could control the lump in his throat, 'why have you left the Tree?'

'The Tree, alas, is no longer standing. Soon after daylight men came with saws and hatchets and cut it down, cut down *our* Tree which has been our home for so long and in which we have reared so many families!'

'That is terrible,' groaned Dodder. 'It was enough the Folly should go, but our Tree!'

But the Folly still lived. Even Man cannot kill a stream. That bright water, which burst from the earth and seemed its very life-blood, flowed still, though down another channel, a man-made channel of bolted iron, where no trees could grow and no voles or gnomes could live. Imprisoned it was, away from the sunlight and the open air. No longer could it reflect the pale blue skies of spring, no longer would the swallows dip into it chattering joyously, but still it flowed, albeit asleep.

A sudden mourning cry floated out over the darkling fields, 'Booo Hooooo! Booo Hooooo!' And then the two dark moth-like birds wheeled away and the gnomes retraced their steps to the dinghy.

Without a word they got in and sorrowfully rowed back to the *Jeanie Deans* and the darkness of the Willow Root engulfed them.

The gnomes and owls were not the only ones who were shifting quarters. Later that night, as Dodder was smoking his pipe close by the Willow Root, he heard the sky above him full of wings. But they were not birds fleeing from the dead Folly, they were the advance guards of that mighty army of spring migrants who were pouring into

Britain at the rate of countless thousands an hour. And he knew that whatever the future had in store for them, the winter at least had gone.

Always the gnomes watched and waited for this night, the night of the Spring Flying as they called it, and greatly cheered and excited, Dodder called the others out. They stood there with Squirrel on the river bank, gazing up into the soft night sky, their long ears pricked. Gnomes have the keenest hearing of any living thing, and their ears told them all that was going on overhead. They could see nothing, but as they listened they heard a faint rustling and soft whispering which, could we but hear it, is one of the most thrilling sounds in the world. For hours on end it went on until, tired and weary with all their strenuous work, the gnomes went back into the tree. And as they fell asleep they still heard the rustling multitudes passing in endless waves high above them.

As soon as it was light they were up and out to meet their friends whom they had not seen for six long months. Before long they heard the voice of Chiffchaff, one of those dainty leaf-tinted warblers, slender of leg and trim of body who are the first to arrive in spring. And he was tired, for he had met bad weather in the Bay of Biscay. Others had come from Algeria and Morocco.

The bird snapped up a small green caterpillar and sang a short burst of song. 'You seem very happy, Chiffchaff,' said Dodder. 'I wish we were!'

'What's the worry? Don't let these Mortals bother you. They've never done much for us anyway, though they're mighty inquisitive. My sister had one of her babies ringed last year.'

'Ringed?' asked Dodder with horror in his face. 'What a dreadful experience!'

Chiffchaff laughed. 'Oh, it didn't hurt the youngster, I suppose, but it was very interfering of them, shoving a band round its leg like that, can't see the point of it. Anyway, don't let's talk of Mortals. How's yourself?'

Poor Dodder told the chiffchaff all their troubles but the merry little bird made light of them. 'Look at us!' he said. 'Look at us chiffchaffs, how we travel, there's nothing in it! I say, have winter quarters and then, when spring comes, go somewhere else! I've tried summering in other countries, but there's nothing to touch this little island.'

Cloudberry, who had been listening with all his ears, nodded briskly. 'Just what *I* tell them, why stick in one place all your life? Move around, see the world!'

'But we haven't wings,' said Dodder, glancing at Cloudberry, 'so don't talk a lot of sparrow gossip.'

'You don't know how nice it is to be back,' went on the chiffchaff. 'For weeks we've had nothing but desert, sand, blue skies and sun, sun, sun, until we were sick of it! We made landfall last night, just after dark, and wasn't it good to smell this country and the green grass and woodlands! You ought to see the Spring Flying,' added the bird, 'you'd never forget it.'

'I've seen it,' said Cloudberry, eagerly bending forward, 'I went to—'

'*Cloudberry!*' warned Dodder, in his 'shut-up' voice, 'that's enough!'

The chiffchaff yawned (a bird yawns by opening its beak wide and waggling its tongue; if you don't believe me, notice a canary yawn) and continued, 'We passed a lot of willow warblers on the way across, they'll be here

pretty soon, in fact I think I hear one now, listen!' And
he was right, for, from a little copse not far away came
the dying fall of the willow warbler's song. 'There!' he
exclaimed, 'what did I tell you? In a week's time they'll be
all over the place. Ah!' said the bird, gazing contentedly
around him at the opening leaves and green fields, '*what* a
green. D'you know, this is what I've been missing for
the last six months, the *green* of England! I think it's the
green that makes us come back here, the green and your
soft grey skies; of course,' the bird added proudly, 'we are
British birds, as we breed here; not like the Heaven
Hounds and the fieldfares and redwings. And that reminds
me, if you could ever see the Autumn Flying, why, that's
even more exciting than the Spring Flying! I don't know
why it is, perhaps it's because a lot of our children are with
us and they've never seen Africa, or Spain, and their
excitement is infectious in a manner of speaking. Don't
you ever get restless, gnomes, when all this (the bird
indicated the fresh greens all around them) when all *this* is
getting tired and dusty and brown, and mists begin to
hang over the water-meadows and the sunlight goes all
pearly and yellow?'

Dodder thought a moment before replying. In some
ways Chiffchaff's words had taken his mind back to an
autumn Folly, with yellow leaves floating on its dark
breast, of lonely camps up there in the higher reaches, and
of the cold dew-wet nights and starlings' chatter.

'Perhaps we do, Chiffchaff, but as we have no wings,
what's the use? All we can do is to go to sleep when the
weather gets very bad.'

'*Go to sleep!*' cried Chiffchaff, in astonishment. '*Sleep?*
Why, you can't enjoy yourself when you're asleep! As it

is, we birds have to sleep, of course, at night, and we live for six or seven Cuckoo Years, if we're lucky, perhaps even a little longer than that. I had a grandmother who lived to be nine Cuckoo Years. And that reminds me,' went on the bird, 'you gnomes are always a bit of a puzzle to us, how old *are* you? We tree warblers often talk about it, some say one thing, some another.'

Dodder looked rather amused. 'Even I don't know that, Chiffchaff. I watched the Folly Oak grow up from a young sapling. That was in the days of King Henry the Sixth. Oh dear—what changes I've seen! The country has changed and the people have changed; they used to dress in such a queer way and the men wore their hair long. But even in those days there was a mill up the Folly and the stream has never altered. Sometimes it's shifted its course a yard or two, but its voice has always been with us, day and night. And now to think the Oak has gone too, it's terrible!'

Dodder buried his face in his hands and Chiffchaff felt very uncomfortable. 'Come, Dodder, that's no way to carry on during the Spring Flying. One day there will be another oak tree and the Folly will run again. Look! the sun's breaking through the woods; in a day or so the cuckoo will be here. And as for me, I must be off to find some caterpillars. I'm mighty hungry, I can tell you.' And away flitted the merry little bird between the green leaves.

CHAPTER FOUR

Plans

'e must make a plan, a sound plan, of what we are going to do.' Dodder, puffing a fragrant cloud of tobacco smoke, leant his elbows on the cabin table.

For over a week they had remained in the Willow Root, recuperating from their ordeal. The fishing in this new river had been marvellous, too marvellous, for as it was such a deep river the fish were correspondingly big and their fishing tackle was repeatedly broken.

And you can imagine their joy when they found that Ben and his wife also took up their abode in the willow!

There was a cavity in the top which gave them shelter. It was the gnomes who had suggested to the Bens that they should keep together as long as possible, despite the buffetings of fate.

Dodder blew another cloud of smoke and regarded Cloudberry with a jaundiced eye. The latter was sure to suggest something absurd, such as going to Spitzbergen or some rubbish and these last few days he had been very full of himself.

'What about asking the Bens down into the cabin?' suggested Squirrel. 'They're up above, we've only to call 'em. Let's have a real powwow.'

'Good idea!' said Dodder. 'Ask 'em down.'

Whilst Baldmoney went on deck, Sneezewort lit the lamp and pulled the curtains, for it was almost dusk.

'I hope they haven't gone out hunting yet,' said Cloudberry, twiddling one end of his beard between finger and thumb. 'Not they,' said Dodder, 'they never wake up until it's almost dark.' Just then steps were heard on the companion-way and Baldmoney appeared followed by Mr and Mrs Ben.

The two birds could only just get into the cabin and Ben bumped his head on the doorway as he came in and uttered a hoot of pain.

'Sorry, Ben!' said Dodder. 'You should read the notice,' and he pointed to a neatly written 'Mind Your Head!' on a square of birch bark nailed to the wall.

'I'm afraid we can't offer you anything to eat or drink,' said the hospitable Dodder, glancing round towards the galley stove. 'I hope you haven't hurt yourself.'

'Oh, that doesn't matter,' said Ben; rubbing his head with his hairy claw. 'I ought to be more careful. Anyway, the house upstairs (he meant in the willow top) is pretty small, I'm always doing it.'

'You've got a cosy place here and no mistake,' said Mrs Ben, looking round the cabin with a professional eye.

'Yes, it's not a bad old tub,' said Dodder, secretly very pleased.

'About the best ship ever built, I should say,' said Ben, glancing admiringly at the pictures and the neat bunks.

'Yes, she's a good well-found ship,' said Baldmoney, 'and I may be able to mend the engines. Truth to say I haven't had a moment yet, what with one thing and another.'

'Of course not,' said Ben understandingly.

'Well, we asked you down here,' began Dodder, drawing up his chair a little closer to the table, 'because we thought as we're all in the same boat we should make some plans as to the future. It's pretty plain we can't stay in this tree; it isn't suitable, for one thing, and besides, there's not room for you, and we do want you to be with us as long as possible.'

'That's very kind of you, Dodder,' said Ben, greatly moved. 'We take that as a great compliment, we do indeed. After all, we've lived long enough together to know each other's little ways.'

And then he looked rather confused. 'You see, Dodder, the whole thing is rather complicated. We always, as you know, have a family every spring. My wife had already laid her eggs in the Oak Tree when those unspeakable savages came and cut it down. Well, we've lost those precious eggs, (here Mrs Ben gave a sniff and turned away her head) and my wife thought of starting up house in the willow here. But I tell her to be reasonable; there's not room and for many reasons it's *quite* unsuitable for a nursery. But you know what females are . . . '

'I know,' said Dodder (he didn't in the least) and Ben went on, 'She will be miserable if we don't have our family as we always have done.'

'Well, why not go around a bit and find a better tree somewhere downstream and then we'll come along too,' Baldmoney suggested.

Here Cloudberry, who had been very fidgety, broke in, 'No, I don't agree with that,' he said, very red in the face. 'I don't think it's any good settling down again in another tree somewhere; we aren't a lot of cabbages. Why can't we go on down to the sea and live in a cave? We might even go off overseas every autumn with the swallows and come back in the spring. I say, let's see the world a bit!'

'Don't be absurd, Cloudberry,' snapped Dodder, banging the table with his fist. 'How can we go with the swallows? They can't carry us on their backs. Preposterous!'

'Absurd!' said Baldmoney.

'Ridiculous suggestion!' grunted Squirrel.

'Well,' said Ben, trying to calm everyone down, for tempers were rising, 'it isn't too easy to find a suitable tree, not so easy as you think, gnomes. What the wife and I don't know about hollow trees isn't worth knowing, though I say it myself, and to find a tree on the river bank with a hole for me and a hole for you will be a most difficult job. We might have to go miles before we found the right one. Take this willow for instance. You've got no storage chambers, you've got to live aboard the *Jeanie*

Deans, and as you know, there isn't room to swing a mouse upstairs. It's very difficult, it is indeed,' and he wagged his big head woefully.

'I know all that, Ben,' said Dodder. 'If the worst comes to the worst then you must find a tree *near* us, and we'll live in another place.'

'Oh dear, it *is* a business house-hunting at our time of life.'

'I don't see what's the point of worrying like this,' said Cloudberry again. 'Why on earth you *want* to settle down at all beats me! I'm all for the wandering life, I am.'

'No!' said Dodder with feigned surprise. 'I should never have thought it of you, Cloudberry!' he added with bitter sarcasm.

'Oh yes I am,' rejoined Cloudberry, who was rather dense and did not see the gleam in Dodder's eye. 'I'm all for the roving life and the wind on the heath.' And to everybody's shocked surprise he burst into the following song, beating time with his snail-shell tankard:

> '*Oh I'm a rover, roving free*
> *The wind in the wood is the wind for me,*
> *The silvery downs and the silver sea.*
> *Heigh-ho for the life of a rover!*'

When Cloudberry had finished there was an icy silence. Then Dodder turned to the owls. 'I must apologize for our brother, Bens, he's never been the same since he met the Heaven Hounds.'

'I haven't,' said Cloudberry at once, and with pride in his voice. 'Nobody ever is! Once you've been with the wild geese there's something gets into your blood.' His eyes were all dreamy now and the others half thought he was going to burst into song again. 'Think of it!' he continued. 'Even now the Heaven Hounds are setting out. I can see them massing in their vast armies on the sand banks, I can hear the bell buoys clanging, I can smell the sea and hear the creamy whispering tide breaking on the leagues of shore. To the north! To the north! *That's* the Great Call which brooks no denying!' He got up and began to pace restlessly round the cabin until Dodder, with a quick movement, seized him by the slack of his skin breeches. Then began a most disorderly riot. Baldmoney jumped up and Squirrel too, Sneezewort caught hold of one leg and Dodder seized the other and in a moment or two the pandemonium was terrible. The table was overturned, Ben and his wife were twice knocked over. The lamp fell down and went out, emitting a stink of smoky oil and you never saw such a disgraceful scene in all your life. 'Lock him in the fo'castle!' gasped Dodder as he struggled to get hold of Cloudberry's collar. At last, the unhappy Cloudberry, completely overpowered, was carried, kicking, up the companion-way and thrust into the fo'castle, where they locked him in. There he set up a terrific din, beating on the door and calling everyone, Ben included, a lot of mouldy cabbages.

'Phew!' said Dodder, when peace reigned once more and everything had been put to rights. 'Now we can perhaps talk in comfort without that silly little idiot upsetting everything and everyone. I must apologize again, Bens, for such a scene, we don't know what's come over Cloudberry, he used to be so peaceable and sensible.'

Ben said it was all right and that he quite understood, but both birds looked rather awkward. Family rows before guests are always nasty ill-bred things.

'As I see it,' said Ben at last, 'this question of settling down in another tree is a very, very difficult question. And I'm going to say something which may surprise, even hurt you, Dodder. To my notion I can see there is something more in Cloudberry's restlessness than we think. The truth is, this England of ours is not what it used to be. Look at all these thunder birds and cars which are flying about all over the place. No, England's getting less and less a place for people like us. If only we could find some other country, a nice quiet country, mind, where we could stay until the Mortals stop cutting down all the trees, and spoiling the countryside. I've no doubt things will come all right again one day and England will be her old self again. But as the world is now, it's no place for the likes of us.'

There was dead silence in the cabin. In some queer way Dodder thought Ben had played them a scurvy trick.

'Mind,' said Ben, noticing the cloudy looks of his companions, 'I'm not siding with Cloudberry, don't think that; but a snipe once told me that away to the west there's a green little island, a lot smaller than Britain, a green, quiet little island, with leagues of wild country, mountains and forest, bogs and lakes. If we went there we should find peace and quietness for the rest of our lives.'

'And how far is this island you're talking about?' said Dodder. 'This wonderful place where we should find peace at last?'

'That I don't know,' replied Ben, 'but I will tell you of somebody who knows *all* about it, for he's been there quite a lot, and that's Woodcock.'

'Woodcock!' exclaimed Dodder. 'What, that comfortable old long-nosed bird?'

'The same,' said Ben, inclining his head gravely. 'Woodcock knows it well, he'll tell you all there is to know about it.'

'And where can we find Woodcock?' asked Dodder. 'At this time of year I seldom see him.'

'I think I can find him,' said Ben. 'I saw him last week in Red Shoot Wood. You wouldn't know the place I expect, it's some way off. I'll go there tonight, if you like, and fetch him along.'

'By all means,' said Dodder, 'find him if you can, and we'll hear what he has to say. If there really is such a place I'd be the last to stick out against our going there—if we *can*,' he added significantly, with a glance at Baldmoney.

'If I mended the engines we could go there,' suggested Baldmoney, 'if it isn't too far.'

'I'm afraid it's a long way,' said Ben. 'A lot farther than your journey up the Folly, and you'd have to cross the sea.'

'That would be easy,' cried Baldmoney, unable to suppress a strange new excitement welling within him. 'If once we got the engine going the *Jeanie Deans* would go anywhere, even to this precious Spitzbergen place that Cloudberry is always babbling about.'

Not many hours later they heard Ben hooting in the distance and in a little while he appeared, in company with the strangest-looking little bird you ever saw. He was dumpy and had a very long nose. His great black eyes were almost as big as Ben's, set very high in a tall forehead. Indeed, he was not unlike Ben in many ways and his dress was a beautiful blend of russet and grey, exactly like the autumn leaves.

'I've found him,' said Ben triumphantly, ushering the bewildered bird into the cabin. 'I thought I could.'

The Woodcock stood blinking in the light of the cabin lamp.

'Welcome, Woodcock,' said Dodder, anxious to put their new guest at his ease. 'This is Baldmoney, this is Sneezewort, and this is Squirrel. Our other brother is a little—er—unwell, excitable, you know.' The last remark was well borne out by a distant confused racket from the direction of the fo'castle.

'Better go and let him out,' said Dodder in an aside to Baldmoney, 'he'll *have* to meet Woodcock anyway.'

Baldmoney stole out of the cabin and soon reappeared with Cloudberry, who now seemed very subdued.

When all the introductions had been made, Ben turned to Woodcock.

'My friends want to know all about that green island where you live,' said Ben. 'You see, they—we, I mean— have lost our home because those hateful Mortals have drained the Folly and the Oak Tree House has been cut down. We haven't a roof over our heads. We thought if we could reach this island of yours we should be able to live in peace, without danger of any more of these disturbances.'

'I can't blame you, I must say,' said the woodcock. 'These Mortals are getting too much above themselves. I'm off tomorrow to my island, and I shall be glad to go. Another day and you wouldn't have found me!'

'Is it a nice *quiet* place?' asked Dodder.

'Quiet! I should say it is!' said Woodcock (and here he

drop his voice), 'I believe there are other gnomes there too, and a few Lantern Men.'

'Why, it must be Ireland you're speaking of,' said Dodder, starting up, 'that's the only place now where any of the Little People remain.'

'Ireland it is,' said the woodcock, lapsing into brogue. 'A fine place it is entirely, green all the year round, as green as spring. And there are oak woods there, and mosses and bogs, and never a mortal comes nigh you, week in, week out. There are streams . . . and the lakes—Oh! the blue of them! And I'm thinking of a place that would suit ye, an island, on a grey, grey loch below the Mourne Mountains. There's an old chapel there, where a hermit lies buried, bless his soul, and a little wood of bog oaks close by. The bracken grows high and the wild geese rest on the shore of it and no sound will you hear but the wind, and the voice of the waves on the shingle!'

Cloudberry, who all this time had been sitting very quiet and composed at the end of the table, began to gulp. He looked nervously at Dodder, at his brothers, and then at Ben. And the latter, to Cloudberry's immense surprise, gave him a prodigious friendly wink.

'It sounds a nice place I must say,' said Dodder at last (and Owl gave Cloudberry another wink) 'but how do we get there?'

'Ah! that's the rub,' said the woodcock. 'How do you get there?'

Cloudberry, unable to control his tongue any longer, got to his feet. 'I know!' he exclaimed. 'The Heav—'

'Silence!' roared Dodder. 'Another word from you,

sir, and you'll be locked up in the fo'castle again and live on acorns and water for a week!'

The discomfited Cloudberry subsided like a pricked bubble and gazed reflectively at the table.

'If we could mend the engines of this ship could we get there?' asked Dodder.

The woodcock gazed round at the cabin. Then he shook his long bill. 'I fear not, good gnomes, the Irish sea would sink this little boat like a pebble.'

Cloudberry opened his mouth again to say something, thought better of it, and continued to gaze at the table in a profound manner.

Then Ben spoke up. 'If I may make a suggestion,' said he, 'did not your brother Cloudberry here go all the way to Spitzbergen on a goose's back last year?'

'To Spitzbergen!' gasped the woodcock, gazing at Cloudberry with unmistakable respect. 'Why, that's *much* farther than Ireland, much farther.'

'You may speak,' said Dodder to Cloudberry, 'but confine your observations to the mode of travel and not to your adventures.'

'I travelled with the Heaven Hounds, as Mr Ben here has just informed you,' said Cloudberry, crimson with pride in spite of himself. 'I met them up the Folly and the Leader of the Skein took me on his back. A cold journey it was, but a comfortable one. And I had the good fortune to be of great use to the——'

'Silence!' commanded Dodder. 'That is all we want to know. You may sit down.'

'The Heaven Hounds left yesterday,' said the woodcock, 'I saw them flying, flying like a great arrow, over Red Shoot Wood. You are too late, my friends, to think of asking them. Anyway,' he added, 'they would never go out of their way to take you to my country. When the Call comes we birds have to go, to the place of our birth. Those Heaven Hounds, which took your brother to Spitzbergen, would be the Pink Feet which rarely visit Ireland. It is the White Fronts who go there and they too will have left by now, I have no doubt. Where this river joins the Severn Sea, the White Fronts live—in winter that is—along the marshes by the Estuary. But as I say they will be leaving now, they will most certainly have gone by the time you reach the Severn, if ever you get that far.'

'Then we have missed our chance,' said Cloudberry, his eyes filling with tears and the great undreamt of hope, which had been rising within him, cruelly dashed.

'Not by any means,' said Baldmoney. 'We have been helped in the past, we shall be helped again. To Ben here, and Mrs Ben, the journey presents no difficulty. And besides,' he added, his eyes glinting, 'I have one of my Ideas. I think we can get over the difficulty of transit.'

Dodder, sitting with head sunk in his hands, sniffed and a little groan escaped him.

'I suppose you all *are* right,' he said in a low voice, 'I suppose we *must* go, somehow or another. And now Brother Baldmoney has one of his "Ideas" there will be no peace for any of us!'

'Cheer up!' said the woodcock. 'All will be well!' He turned to go. 'I shall expect to see you there,' he said. 'I will tell Ben what compass course to steer for that little island that I spoke of. He will no doubt be your pilot, whether you fly or sail there. As for me, I must be off, I'm late already!' And with a polite bow, the strange little bird walked up the companion-way with the Bens closely following on his heels, and vanished from view.

In the following breathless silence, poor old Dodder, weary with years and feeling more tired than he had ever been before in his long life, heaved a deep, deep sigh.

CHAPTER FIVE

Mr Shoebottom's Boy

hatever 'Idea' Baldmoney had in that wise little head of his he kept it to himself. But in the days following the round table conference just related he spent most of his time down in the engine room, hammering and scraping at the springs and bolts.

The others were not sorry. After a promising spell of warm spring-like days there was much rain and frost at night and everyone, even Cloudberry, was glad that they were not somewhere downriver at the mercy of the wintry weather.

Baldmoney was so busy he had his meals taken down to him in the engine-room by Sneezewort. The others spent their time fishing and making some very smart and serviceable coats out of the moleskins which Ben had given them. Mrs Ben was very impressed when she saw the finished garments.

Squirrel became venturesome. He made 'excursions' downriver all by himself. One day, not half-a-mile below their temporary home, he came upon a road which led to a village. Close to the river was a bridge and a garage-cum-shop which belonged—according to the notice over the garage door—to a gentleman named Shoebottom. The notice said 'G. Shoebottom, Garage. Petrol, oils, quick repairs of all kinds undertaken.' Shoebottom had a small son and a very fat black spaniel called 'Bogie', which looked more like a woolly roly-poly bolster than a dog. This animal chased Squirrel up an apple tree one afternoon and had not Mr Shoebottom been busy in his engineering shop and the little Shoebottom at school, things might have gone hardly with him. He was lucky to escape and thereafter he avoided that section of the river bank.

And then the cold bleak weather changed. Mid-April came, and with it a spell of warm days which made everyone feel that it was real summer at last. The swallows came, and the cuckoo, and every plant and leaf grew apace. Poor old Ben had a very trying time with Mrs Ben, for the latter, now that the countryside was so full of such green promise, pined for another family. But old Ben knew best; as he often told her, 'Ben knows best', and after a day or two she decided that she would wait until the following spring. Everyone knew that great things were brewing and those days were just as full of suppressed excitement as when Baldmoney and Sneezewort were planning their trip up the Folly.

This new river was full of surprises and in many ways was much more imposing than their old beloved Folly.

But for all that it did not have the same dear intimacy of that other little stream and even Dodder confessed to himself that they could *never* be happy on its banks, even if Ben were to discover a suitable tree. There was another thing: sometimes boats came up the river, boats with Mortals in them, who played gramophones and threw ginger-beer bottles into the water and left paper lying about. Loving couples often came by, with a dreamy look in their eyes and once a noisy grunting motor launch passed the Willow and its wash came slooping and slopping under the root with such force that it nearly swamped the *Jeanie Deans*. And I must confess that their neighbours were very stand-offish. Of course there were voles and rabbits in dozens, living quite near, but they never dropped in for a friendly chat. No, it did not take long for even Dodder to realize they could never be happy in this sophisticated waterway.

But though the sun shone now with such warmth and the days were full of birdsong and glorious light, and buttercups by the million began to deck the water meadows, Baldmoney, working away in the bowels of the ship, did not seem to be making any headway.

One evening he came into the cabin looking very weary and strained. He flopped down and stared gloomily at his brothers.

'What's up, Baldmoney?' asked Dodder kindly. 'We haven't worried you at all at your work, have we? We've kept out of your way as much as possible.'

'I can't mend that blessed spring,' confessed Baldmoney, with a break in his voice. 'I'm afraid I shall never be able to, the job's beyond me.'

'Oh, cheer up, Baldmoney, don't take on so. Supposing

we push off and drift; after all we came down from the Big Sea that way.'

'You don't understand,' said Baldmoney. 'We could never drift down to the sea, it's miles and miles and *miles*—forty, fifty times the distance we covered up the Folly!'

'Oh dear me,' said Dodder, looking very worried. 'I never knew it was as far as that. How do *you* know?'

'King of Fishers told me last week. He said we might do it if we could mend the engine, but even then it's going to take all summer. Without the engine we haven't a hope and, besides, the boat isn't under control.'

'I see,' said Dodder. 'Then we shall have to stay here. But you said you had an Idea the other day. What was it?'

'I'm not going to tell anyone,' said Baldmoney. 'Ben knows my secret, but he's promised not to tell. You see, I've talked the whole thing out quietly with him and he agrees entirely with my Plan. But unless we can mend the engine we can't put it into operation, if you understand me.'

'It's a bad business. I don't know what to suggest, unless we go on foot,' said Dodder after a pause.

'That's impossible,' said Baldmoney. 'You *know* it is, Dodder. How could *you* walk for miles and miles, it just can't be done.'

'What about Sir Herne? Can't he help?' suggested Dodder. 'He gave me a lift upstream, you remember.'

'No, Sir Herne won't leave the district, not even for us. Herons don't hold with flying about the country; besides, even he couldn't take us all on his back.'

Dodder looked glumly through the porthole at a

moorhen which was swimming past with a train of sooty moor-chicks following after. He sighed and passed his hand over his brow wearily.

'Well, don't let's worry, Baldy, old fellow; everything will come right, you see.'

Those lovely days of spring seemed to mock our poor homeless gnomes and their good friend Squirrel. Cloudberry, irritated at Baldmoney's failure to mend the engine, was more restless than ever, and spent much of his time teasing the water voles and aimlessly wandering along the river bank, despite the warnings of the others.

One hot afternoon in early May when Sneezewort, Dodder, and Baldmoney were playing Acorn Hop on the cabin table (Acorn Hop is rather like draughts but much more complicated) something very distressing happened.

Cloudberry was, as usual, 'mucking about' downriver in the dinghy (strictly against Dodder's orders) and Squirrel had been persuaded by that restless spirit to go with him.

Dodder had just taken one of Baldmoney's best pieces on the Acorn Hop board when there was a sudden noise outside. They heard the dinghy crash into their port side and a second later Squirrel and Cloudberry, very out of breath and pale of face, came tumbling down the companion-way. 'Quick, quick, they're after us. Get up inside the tree or we'll all be caught!'

'Whatever's the matter?' exclaimed Dodder, starting up. 'Is it stoats or wood-dogs?'

'Neither,' said Squirrel, 'but I tell you if we stay down here we'll all be caught like minnows in a bottle. Come on, all of you, we'll tell you later.' Without giving any further information Squirrel and Cloudberry ran up the stairs again and disappeared on deck. In no more time than it takes to tell, Dodder, Baldmoney, and Sneezewort followed. By standing on the bridge it was possible for them to scramble up inside the tree, for there was a hollow slit which went up the interior for some way.

They had hardly pulled themselves up when a terrific barking began outside, a perfectly deafening noise. And a moment later the head of a fat black spaniel pushed into the opening below them, sending big waves slopping about on the red roots.

'Gercher!' chattered Squirrel. 'Get out, you brute!' and picking off a lump of rough wood aimed it at the spaniel. The dog could only get its head and shoulders into the hole, so it swam about, barking watery barks and glaring up at them with bloodshot eyes. It ignored the *Jeanie Deans* which kept bumping its nose.

'This is what comes of you playing about in daylight,' growled Dodder. 'I told you not to go out until dusk.'

'I couldn't help it,' said Cloudberry feebly. 'Squirrel and I went for a row downriver and this beastly dog jumped out of the rushes at us and what's more serious still, one of the young Shoebottoms heard the noise and he's coming along the bank with another urchin to see what all the noise is about.'

Dodder groaned as if in pain. 'I'm surprised at you, Squirrel, I wouldn't have thought *you'd* be so silly.'

Squirrel hung his head sulkily. 'That dog's chased me before—I hate him,' he muttered in his whiskers.

'Well,' Dodder observed, 'we can only hope he gives up and goes away. Once we get Mortals on our track there'll be trouble.'

But the dog had no intention of going away. It could smell and see Squirrel squeezed up in the dark tree and he could see the gnomes too. So he swam round and round, barking as if he were quite mad.

Very soon they heard hobnailed boots clambering and knocking on the tree. They also heard Ben and his wife fly out and then a voice called, 'Come on, Winkle, 'ere's an owl's nest up 'ere an' Bogie's got an otter in the tree!'

The gnomes heard the boys climb up to the top of the willow and a lot of dust came down. But they found no eggs, only a quantity of beetle castings, and after a while they climbed down again and began poking with a stick under the hollow beneath.

The young Shoebottom poked so vigorously that he severed the cable attaching the *Jeanie Deans* to the inside of the root and the next moment the very worst possible thing happened. The ship, free of her anchor rope, slowly moved out from the hollow and floated in full view of the two urchins on the bank.

'Now we're finally and *utterly* sunk!' said Dodder, white with rage. 'Thanks to you, Cloudberry, we've lost the *Jeanie Deans*. I've a good mind to drown you or throw you down to that beastly dog!' The 'beastly dog' was still swimming around and barking. Then came a squeal of ecstatic delight.

'OOOh! Wot a loverly boat—'ere Winkle, cum an' look at this loverly boat wot's cum out from unner the tree!'

They saw a crooked claw reach out and grasp the *Jeanie Deans* by the foremast and in a brace of shakes the ship was lifted out of their ken and below them there was nothing but agitated ripples, rocking to and fro and sucking at the willow roots. The expressions of delight which echoed all about them fully testified that the *Jeanie Deans* was meeting with huge approval.

''Ere, let me wind 'er up, there's a key in 'ere,' they heard one urchin squeal.

'The spring's broke, but ain't she a loverly ship!'

'Coo, there's a lil' cabin an' all, full o' things, tables an' all!'

'Coo!'

''Ere, let *me* look.'

'Get out, I found it first!'

'Garn, that you didn't, Bogie found it. If 'e 'adn't gone in after the otter you wouldn't 'ave found it, so there!'

'I should!'

'You wouldn't now!'

There was a sound of a scuffle in which the dog, tiring of trying to get at the gnomes and Squirrel in the tree, apparently joined. Then the wrangling died away. Scrambling down the tree the gnomes peeped through a bunch of stinging nettles. The two boys were going away down the river bank, the little Shoebottom carrying the *Jeanie Deans* in his arms. Dodder watched them out of sight and without a word he went back and sat down on the willow root with his head in his hands.

Cloudberry and Squirrel (the latter especially) appeared very shame-faced and said nothing, so Baldmoney and Sneezewort went over to Dodder and tried to comfort him.

Why was fate so cruel to these poor little refugees? What wrong had they done? Now their last home had gone and with it everything they possessed: their fishing rods, Dodder's precious wines, their moleskins, all their worldly goods and it was all Cloudberry's fault.

To mock them the swallows swept overhead twittering so happily, speeding cloud shadows raced each other over the green hedges and larks sang their silver songs high above the spring corn. In the reed thickets by the waterside the sedge warblers sang and gnats danced in the sunlight.

Where was Pan? What was he doing to let such a thing happen? Was he somewhere close by, hidden among the silvery willows which bent so gracefully before the breeze of evening?

As a matter of fact, quite unknown to the gnomes and Squirrel, he *was* close by, secreted among the willow thickets, smiling to himself, a queer crooked smile as he toyed with his pipe. He had arranged the whole thing. He put the idea of a row into Cloudberry's silly head, he had lured the spaniel to hunt for water-rats along the river bank, he had planned that the little Shoebottom and his friend should play truant that afternoon from school. And all this goes to show, as you will very soon see, what a wise old Pan he was!

CHAPTER SIX

Mr Shoebottom's Shop

here was a starling whistling up in the willow tree. His plumage was shot with lovely blues, greens, purples, and reds, a coat of many colours. And his song was many-coloured too, little snatches of sound made up on the spur of the moment: sheep bleating, jackdaws chacking, peewits crying, swallows twittering, and sandwiched in, here and there, his own queer clicks and clackings.

An amusing bird, a clown among the birds, Nature's

jester. Many a time had he made the gnomes rock with laughter at his funny ways and pranks. How they loved to see the big starling flocks in autumn, wheeling in a shimmering cloud over the reed beds! How they laughed to see these busy star-spangled people waddling in the meadows after wireworms. But just now, Dodder thought, it was no time for jesting. And after a while, when the starling began to copy the sound of Mr Shoebottom's hammer in his workshop, Dodder could stand it no longer. 'Hi! You there! Shut up, can't you!'

Now the starling had never before been spoken to so rudely by a gnome. He regarded Dodder and his brothers with a shocked and injured air.

'Oh, I'm *sorry*, Spangle, I didn't mean to shut you up, but we've had a dreadful loss.'

The bird gave a shrill whistle, which ascended the scale and then with a throaty gibber came to rest on the grass close by. 'Dear, dear, dear,' said Spangle, regarding the sorrowful group, 'I'm sorry to hear that, I am indeed. What's the trouble?'

'We've lost our boat,' said Baldmoney, and Squirrel and Cloudberry affected to gaze with unusual interest at a large red cow which was pulling at the rush-tops downriver.

'Not the *Jeanie Deans*—the famous *Jeanie Deans*?' said Spangle, and he gave a low whistle. 'Why, we all knew what a lovely boat she was and how you had her safe and sound here in the willow tree. How did it happen?'

'Well, there's no need to go into that now; least said, soonest mended,' said Dodder wearily, 'but she's gone and gone for good. The Shoebottom kid has stolen it!'

The starling was speechless. 'Why, *that* little brat. Goodness gracious, but what a shame! I've cause to know that family well, a good hard-working family too, and they have a nice warm thatch. Why, I've got a wife now sitting on five eggs under their very roof. We build there every year. Old Shoebottom's a good sort, never interferes with me. Says he likes us whistling about his chimneys. Clever bloke too, with his hands, so they say.'

'Clever or not, the brat's got the *Jeanie Deans*,' said Dodder grumpily, 'and I don't know what we're going to do. Even though her spring was broken she made a splendid houseboat.'

Spangle sat for a minute or two regarding the gnomes out of the corner of his eye. The sun was shining and in its bright rays Dodder was struck by the beauty of the bird's plumage. Usually they made fun of the starlings and called them Spangleclowns. 'Tell you what,' said Spangle, 'I'll fly across to the cottage now and see if I can see anything of the boat. There's been a fine old clatter going on in the workshop all afternoon, even my wife remarked on it. Just wait here and I'll be back in a wriggle of wire-worms.'

'He's an amusing fellow is Spangle,' said Baldmoney, after the bird had gone. 'Well-meaning too, but I can't see he can do much to help us.'

In a very short while, however, back came Spangle, and he was fairly bubbling over with excitement.

'Old man Shoebottom's in the workshop right enough, with the kid. I peeped through the window. They've got the *Jeanie Deans* on the bench and they're working away on her like leatherjackets.'

'Ho ho,' said Baldmoney, pricking up his ears. 'They are, are they?'

'True enough,' said the starling. 'If that boat's got a broken spring, as you say she has, old Shoebottom will soon put it to rights. Thinks no end of his kid, you know—nasty little brat, I call it, but there's no accounting for tastes.'

'Now if only we could get that boat out of the workshop tonight,' said Baldmoney, pulling his beard, 'that would be the thing to do.'

'Well,' said Spangle, 'old Shoebottom is a member of the Bowling Club, and I happen to know they've got a dinner on tonight at the Spotted Cow, no end of a beano it's going to be. I heard it from another starling who nests in the roof of the pub up in the village. So he'll be out of the way and he may come back in liquor; he usually does after affairs of that sort. Mrs Shoebottom's a sound sleeper and the brat won't wake. The dog's the only thing to worry about, that and getting the boat out of the shop. It's all locked up at night.'

'Well, this *is* a teaser,' said Baldmoney, who nevertheless had brightened up considerably.

'You'll get into the place all right,' said Spangle. 'The door's an old one, I've even squeezed in myself sometimes to have a look round, but it'll be a job to get the boat out, as you say. Anyway, your friend Ben can keep watch, can't he? He can sit on the gable top and keep a look-out.'

'Yes, he'll do anything to help,' said Dodder, 'but how we're going to get the boat out—that's the question. Supposing we all go down there tonight and have a look, eh? What do you say, Baldmoney?'

'Good idea!'

'And Cloudberry and Squirrel' (those worthies started

guiltily), 'as you've led us into this mess you'll have to do all the dirty work. You'll have to go inside the shop—how I don't know—and see what you can see.'

It was after eleven o'clock that night when the gnomes and Squirrel, accompanied by Ben, set out for the Shoebottom's shop. A full moon rode clear in the sky and a brisk breeze blew ragged clouds across its pallid face.

The trees and hedges had now put on their heavy green and it was eerie to see the leaves bending and swishing under the rough caress of the wind and to see quite big waves breaking on the river banks. It did not take them long to reach the place. Squirrel and Cloudberry, anxious to make good for their earlier behaviour, led the way across the meadows.

Very soon they saw the gleam of the moon on the galvanized roof of the garage. The gnomes trod fearfully. Never before had they been so close to the haunts of men and the smells which assailed them were shocking. Gnomes, as I said in my former book, have a very strong sense of smell and the stinks of petrol, paraffin, grease and what-not, were truly horrible.

The Shoebottoms' house was well curtained, only a faint light showed in a lower window where Mrs Shoebottom was sitting up for her husband.

They stole along the grass beside the road and in a few moments they entered the yard. On the chimney-pot they could see the rigid form of old Ben keeping watch, bobbing up and down as he looked about him on all sides, now towards the village and up the road, now across the windy fields. Nothing escaped that piercing gaze of his.

'It's lucky the dog sleeps in the house,' whispered Cloudberry, 'I found that much out from Spangle. Here's the shop. Look! it's easy to get in; we can squeeze in under the door!'

Squirrel went first, then came Baldmoney and Cloudberry, followed by Dodder and Sneezewort.

The first thing that Sneezewort did when he got inside was to fall headlong over an old 'Lodge' sparking plug which lay on the greasy black floor.

'Clumsy little idiot,' hissed Dodder. 'Look where you're going!'

The moonlight was streaming in through the windows, making the interior of the workshop appear very ghostly.

To Baldmoney's mathematical mind the sight of this place was enthralling. All about lay screws, bolts and pistons, coils of wire, drums of oil, iron bars, cylinder heads, parts of bicycles, two canvas canoes, an anvil, rakes, hammers, nails, gaskets, and Heaven knows what.

It did not take Squirrel long to hop up on the workbench and there, sure enough, was the *Jeanie Deans*. Shoebottom senior had been working late upon it and he had only just got the job done before black-out time.

'Try the key,' whispered Dodder, trembling with excitement, 'you know how it works.' But Squirrel had forgotten and Sneezewort and Cloudberry had to climb up on the bench and help him. From the darkness above Dodder heard them fitting the key and a second later there came a sudden whirr from the propellers.

Now that alarming buzz in that silent ghostly place, patterned as it was by the moonbeams, and full of odd-looking shadows, was too much for Sneezewort. He jumped back and collided with a heavy iron bar which

Shoebottom (or Pan) had propped near the window. With an appalling noise this weighty metal rod crashed down and shivered the panes into a thousand fragments!

For a second everyone was frozen with horror. And then Dodder, whose brain always worked quicker than most folks, realized that their problem had been accidentally solved. The window was broken and through that shattered pane it might be possible to pass the *Jeanie Deans*!

It was only a few feet above the ground, there was a bed of nettles under the window. They could push the boat out and trust to its falling softly outside.

With trembling hands and paws, the gnomes and Squirrel lifted her bows up and pushed with might and main. It took every ounce of their strength to move the ship but the urgency of their mission gave them unwonted power. The *Jeanie Deans* was thrust forward (Baldmoney slipping some bolts under her keel to act as rollers) and the next moment, with a final heave, she toppled from sight into the moonlit night.

But still the job was yet half-done. The problem now was to get her across the road and down to the river, a matter of thirty yards. Again Baldmoney's mathematical brain came to the rescue. He threw the others three of the bolts and after a mighty struggle they got them under her keel and began to move the ship, inch by inch, out of the yard and into the road, Squirrel and Cloudberry pulling on a rope from the bow, and the others pushing behind.

Panting and heaving they edged her along. Success was in sight. But at that moment there came a sudden barking from the house. Bogie the spaniel had heard the crash of glass and the unwonted noises from the garage and was giving the alarm. At that moment too Ben gave a wild hoot and swept low over the yard shouting that old Shoebottom had just turned the corner of the road beyond the bridge. It was a lucky thing that once over the road the ground sloped steeply under some rails to the river's edge. There old Shoebottom had several rowing boats tied up (he let out boats for hire as well as selling petrol) and just as the straining gnomes and Squirrel had pulled the *Jeanie Deans* into the middle of the road Shoebottom, reeling slightly and singing, 'It's my delight' at the top his voice, bore down upon them.

As the tipsy fellow drew near the song died on his lips. He saw clearly in the moonlight four little figures and a rabbit-like creature hauling the boat across his path. 'Hey!' he shouted. 'Hey, you! That's my boat, that is!' But the gnomes had now got the boat on the slope, she rolled and slithered down the bank, and just as Shoebottom came puffing and stumbling right upon them, the *Jeanie Deans* took the water. Dodder and the others had only just time to climb aboard, Squirrel was left behind and forced to swim after them, an arrangement he had not bargained for as the water was icy chill.

A tremendous row now began from the direction of the shop. Mrs Shoebottom rushed out, followed by the yelling dog, and she soon saw the shattered window of the garage.

'Thieves! Thieves!' shouted they all in unison. Old Shoebottom was staggering about in circles, waving his arms and pointing to the river. 'They've made off with our Billy's boat,' he was shouting over and over again.

'Perlice!' yelled Mrs Shoebottom with deafening gusto. 'We've been robbed we have, we've been robbed! Perlice!'

Meanwhile the current was bearing the *Jeanie Deans* out into midstream and the shadows of the trees hid her from Mortal gaze.

In a brace of shakes they got the engine going and without more ado they made off downstream as fast as they could go, despite the frantic squeaks of Squirrel, toiling in the water. That unhappy beast had at length to take to the bank and join them farther down.

It was truly amazing how well their plans had gone. The gnomes were beside themselves with joy. Ben and his wife circled above them against the stars, hooting happily, and away back at the garage Mrs Shoebottom was gently guiding her tipsy husband up the rickety stairs.

'I tells 'ee, Mary, them was *pixies* I saw! Plain as a pikestaff, a-pullin' and a-haulin' that there toy ship over the road!'

And Mrs Shoebottom was saying 'There, there,' and such-like soothing things, and shaking her head from side to side.

''Twas the wind that blew the crowbar through the windy, mi-dear,' she said, ''twas no burglar, that I'm sure.'

'But Billy's boat's gone I tells ye, woman,' her husband kept on repeating in a thick voice, 'an' I saw them little critturs a-carryin' o' it off!'

And up in the thatch a sleepy starling, who had stayed awake to see the fun, clappered his bill and went happily to sleep.

CHAPTER SEVEN

Conversation Piece

 ow the gnomes found themselves once more back in possession of their beloved ship their joy knew no bounds. The unhappy Mr Shoebottom had done his work well and the *Jeanie Deans* was apparently as good as the day Dodder came upon her reposing on the white sand of Poplar Island.

True, she had lost some of her pristine glory, her paintwork had suffered through what she had undergone, but she pulled along through the water with all her old fire and glided as gracefully as any swan upon the ample bosom of this new river. It cannot be expected, or pretended, that the gnomes found her interior fittings as smart as they used to be, nor that they found everything intact. There was some splintered woodwork in the cabin, several panels had suffered, either from the attentions of Master Shoebottom, or from the fall from the garage window. But the clumsy fingers of old Shoebottom had been unable to force an entry into the cabin and even Master Shoebottom had not had the leisure to explore all the hidden treasure below decks.

The wine was untouched, though one shell was broken and the precious liquid had drained away with the bilge water. Also the glass in the pictures was shattered but the pictures themselves were happily undamaged.

Baldmoney soon got busy putting everything to rights, mending the broken panelling and so forth. Even their new moleskin coats were found hanging up in the little cupboard by the bunks quite unharmed.

You may be sure that they put a good many miles between them and the scene of their alarming adventures. They journeyed unceasingly from dusk to dawn and as they went the river widened and widened. Sometimes they passed under bolted railway bridges. Some came aslant to the path of the river, as though they were out of drawing, as the artists say, some were of steel, others were of brick. Once they passed a big town with many bridges and factory chimneys. And once too, a puzzled policeman, yawning on his beat, saw the shadowy outline of the *Jeanie*

Deans pass below him as he stood on a road bridge, but he thought it was a large rat and yawned again and looked eagerly for the dawn.

In passing these Man Dwellings the gnomes were assailed by the many foreign smells which quite swamped the natural smells of reedbed and osier. They were always glad to be past them and out among the open country once again.

They quite lost count of the water mills and villages which went gliding by them. By day they sought the sanctuary of deep osiers, where the wind sang tunes among the slender wands and swallows twittered at close of day. Sometimes they pushed their way into dense reed beds, those graceful slender forests which were ever a-whispering their mysterious secrets to one another and where the little reedy bird people slung their neat ball-like nests anchored from stem to stem.

There was no urgent hurry; when they came to some restful spot, an eyot or backwater, they stayed for a day or so, quietly fishing and now and again having a refreshing swim. For now the country was at its loveliest. Never before had they seen such water-lily beds or such magnificent cup-shaped flowers. Never before had they seen such black poplars, bigger by far than those which they remembered at Moss Mill. And as for the fish they caught—why, Dodder had his tackle broken many times a day by leviathans of the deep, as big or bigger than the perch he caught when he travelled up the Folly. There was no lack of good fresh food. Watercress was abundant and all sorts of tender water salads which Mortals do not know of. How pleasant it was to lie in your bunk and listen to the reed warblers all a-singing, to hear the sweet bell-like voice of the cuckoo sounding across those spacious evening meads. Sometimes oak woods, bluebell floored, came right down to the river's brim, and in those soft summer evenings, delicious with the scent of hayfields and meadowsweet, they watched the big river bats hawking to and fro and heard the monotonous 'crake crake' of land rails among the thick green mowing grass and branching buttercups.

Ben and his wife shadowed them, quiet and watchful ghosts. The two devoted birds were never far away. By day they went to sleep in some thick meadow elm or churchyard yew, but evening always found them floating along the misty river within sight and hail of the *Jeanie Deans*, noting their steady progress.

The gnomes made many new friends in their daily stopping places. The quaint little fluffy corks of dabchicks were a familiar sight, birds who have, as they told Dodder with great pride, no 'parsons' noses', and they met also the graceful and aristocratic crested grebes who glided by with dignified mien. Swans, of course, they met, but these creatures were as vain as peacocks. Once they had an encounter with a particularly bad-tempered bird.

They foolishly anchored near a swan's nest, and in a very short while the cob came alongside and ordered Dodder to move on. 'We don't allow gypsies, land *or* water, on this stretch of river,' he said. Dodder answered with some heat that they had as much right, and more, than he to the river. Whereupon the cob waxed wroth and threatened to drown them and sink the boat. He would have done so had not Dodder, thinking 'discretion the better part of valour', weighed anchor and gone on.

'As spoilt and vain-glorious as the Crow Wood

Chinaman,' was Dodder's verdict, and long after they were out of earshot everyone shouted uncomplimentary remarks to the hissing angry bird.

One beautiful evening late in May they were anchored in a dense bed of reeds surrounding a calm backwater. Lily beds stretched on either hand and blue dragonflies hawked about the stern of the *Jeanie Deans* as keenly as the swallows and martins, which latter birds were seeking for larger game in that quiet retreat close beside the main river.

There is a particular charm about such places. Hidden away by pallisades of graceful whispering reeds and willows one can dream the hours away and nothing but the sleepy twitter of birds or the splash of a fat fish breaks the quietness. Dodder was up on the bridge, contentedly smoking a pipe, his elbows resting on the rail, watching the blue-black swallows and the white spots of the martins' rumps as they weaved about the ship.

Baldmoney and Squirrel were playing Acorn Hop on the foredeck and Cloudberry was fishing over the stern. From the faint clinks and clanks from the galley it appeared that Sneezewort was preparing the evening repast.

'It's quite like old times,' said Baldmoney, sweeping the pieces off the board and leaning on the deck rail. 'Quite like the old days when we were going up the Folly to look for Cloudberry, only we don't seem so hurried now.'

'Yes,' said Squirrel, falling in with Baldmoney's idle mood, 'it's sad we'll never sail the Folly again. We've had some tough times since then. I often wondered what would have happened to me if I'd stayed on in Crow Wood. Not that I ever want to go back there. Seems as if

I've been living along with you fellows all my life somehow.' And he yawned.

'Young Cloudberry seems more contented these days,' said Baldmoney after a while. 'Seems to me he's been more subdued too after that business with the Shoebottoms.'

'Yes, I was a fool to be led on by him like that, but *you* know what he is, and as it turned out it was the best possible thing that could have happened, otherwise we should never have got the spring mended.'

'No,' replied Baldmoney, 'that job was beyond me I must confess, Squirrel. Doesn't it make you think, looking back on it all, that Pan must have engineered the whole thing?'

'P'raps so,' agreed Squirrel. 'There's a lot of things we can't figure out, but plans don't always come out right. Talking of plans, you have a Plan, so Dodder tells me, about getting to Woodcock's island?'

'Oh *that*,' said Baldmoney. 'Yes, I've got a Plan, of sorts; at least, Ben and I have one between us, but we've got to reach the Sea first before we tell anyone about it.'

As Baldmoney talked Squirrel saw him looking very intently at the reeds which swayed about all around them. Squirrel was a very sharp animal and seldom missed much. And this interest of Baldmoney's intrigued him enormously. Now, if he had been a little less subtle he might have remarked upon it, but instead he held his peace and pretended to be watching the swallows curvetting and circling about them. 'Look at the martins and swallows, they're having a high old time just here, catching no end of flies!'

'What about a row in the dinghy?' suggested Baldmoney, ignoring Squirrel's last remark.

'Good idea!' said Squirrel eagerly, who was, truth to say, just a little bored. 'But won't we have to get Dodder's permission?'

'He looks in a good mood,' observed Baldmoney, 'he's always in a good mood on an evening like this and he's smoking a pipe, which is a good sign. I'll give the old chap a hail. Hi! Dodder!'

'Hullo below there! What d'ye want?'

'May Squirrel and I take out the dinghy for a row?'

'What for?'

'Just for a row—we won't go far!'

There was a pause as Dodder took his pipe out of his mouth and pointed the stem at Squirrel. 'No more tricks then, you mustn't go out in the main river.'

'All right,' shouted Baldmoney, 'we won't.'

Full of excitement they lowered the boat into the water—luckily the Shoebottoms had not taken it off the deck davits—and a moment later both were safely aboard and rowing away. 'Don't make too much row,' whispered Baldmoney, 'we don't want Cloudberry bothering to come. I think he's so busy fishing he won't notice us.'

But at that moment Cloudberry, sensing in his uncanny restless way there was fun afoot, called out in his piping voice, 'Hey! come back for me, I'd like a row too!'

'Sorry,' called Squirrel, 'sorry, Cloudberry, old chap, but we can't come back now. Go on, row fast, Baldmoney,' he added in an aside, 'we don't want him with us.'

In a moment or two they had drawn away and were threading between the stout green stems of the reeds and the *Jeanie Deans*, with the gesticulating Cloudberry standing in the stern, was lost to view.

'What fun it is,' said Squirrel, looking about him and settling himself on the cushions, 'this is *real* fun, this is!' and he leant back luxuriously and closed his eyes, sniffing the air, for he could smell the hawthorn wind. There comes a day in early summer when the air becomes charged with the scent of the newly-opened hawthorn flowers. This lovely perfume, not unlike bean flowers, is wafted for miles o'er hill and dale. It needs a warm wind to bring it out and only on one day is it possible to notice it. Mortals sniff and say, 'What a lovely smell, what can it be?' That is the wind that the Little People name the hawthorn wind.

After a while, when they had pushed well into the reed bed, Baldmoney stopped rowing. He pulled the little dinghy against one of the stout stems and began cutting at it with his knife.

'What's the idea?' asked Squirrel, watching his friend with interest.

'Oh, I just want to test out something,' said Baldmoney. He hacked away at the stout reed stem and in a minute or two its feathery top trembled and it toppled across the prow like a falling tree.

Baldmoney worked away and soon cut off a length. This was, of course, hollow and quite strong. Baldmoney examined it with care, shaking his head now and again, and passing low remarks, hardly audible to Squirrel. 'Not strong enough by half . . . wouldn't stand the strain, no . . . they won't do at all . . . must find something else . . . ' and suchlike observations which so tickled Squirrel's curiosity that he could contain himself no longer.

'Whatever *are* you about, Baldmoney, muttering away like that? Do tell me. Is it something to do with that Plan of yours?'

'P'raps it is, p'raps it isn't,' said Baldmoney mysteriously. 'They're no good anyway, not strong enough.'

'Not strong enough for *what*?'

'For my purpose.'

'Oh, all *right*,' said Squirrel testily, 'I don't want to know your precious secret, but I think you might tell me!'

But Baldmoney would not be drawn.

He lay back and paddled slowly along with half-shut eyes. 'This is the sort of thing I just enjoy,' he murmured, gently guiding the dinghy between two water-lily leaves, 'just gliding about like this. What huge fun we're having.' He sighed again.

'I believe Dodder is keeping a log every night,' said Squirrel, 'ever since we started from the Oak Tree he's kept a diary.'

'All captains have to keep a log,' said Baldmoney. 'Surely you know that? The trouble is, Squirrel, I'm no hand at writing myself, engineering's more in my line. I say,' he cried, half sitting up, 'what a jolly place we're coming to!'

They had glided out of the reed bed into another smaller backwater. It really *was* the most fairy-like place, with the dark green water studded with pure white lilies, each with a yellow centre, a small pool not more than ten yards across.

The willows, in a lovely silver tangle, formed a wall on all sides, shutting out the distant views of river and meadows. The low sunbeams, pouring down into that well-like place were gilding the tops of the bushes but the water itself was in cool shade. All manner of beautiful riverside flowers grew among the reeds and vegetation:

willow herb, milk parsley, water betony and dock, and many another moisture-loving plant; each added its quota of scent, which lay heavily on the evening air.

From under some water-lily leaves they saw the trembling tails of several large fishes. To fish, the flat lily leaves were like parasols.

Waterhens swam about very busily, but when they saw the boat appear they shyly took refuge in the reed pallisades and passed watery remarks to one another.

'Now, if we had only brought our fishing lines,' said Squirrel, 'we might have caught some of those big fellows hiding under the lily pads there.'

'Oh, it's too hot, even to fish,' murmured Baldmoney, yawning widely and letting the little boat bump gently among the lilies. 'I believe I'm enjoying this trip more than the one we had up the Folly. Hullo! See who comes!'

Squirrel turned about and saw, high above them, the huge extended vanes of grey wings, the pinions spread like fingers. It was Sir Herne the heron. He wheeled round in a wide arc and seeing the little opening below he checked himself and plunged down at a surprising speed, almost as if he had been shot. They could hear the still air burring through his feathers. When he came just above them they saw his long green legs suddenly drop down and he alighted with infinite grace a few yards away on a half-submerged willow root. It was quite remarkable to see how his silver-grey plumage toned with the willows all about them.

'Sir Herne!' exclaimed Baldmoney, and doffed his cap politely. Squirrel, having no cap to take off, bowed distantly.

'Hey ho! if it isn't the gnomes again! Why, I haven't seen any of you since I gave your friend Dodder a lift up the Folly, let me see . . . how long ago was that? Last summer, wasn't it?'

'Yes, he was following after us and he told us how good you'd been,' said Baldmoney, beaming broadly.

'But, gnomes, what *has* happened to you? I've been thinking a lot about you lately. All the Stream People have left the Folly and the stream is dry. Your tree is down too. You wouldn't recognize the place. But I said to myself, I'll bet a pound roach to an ounce minnow the gnomes have not been caught napping, I'll wager they've gone off in that boat of theirs I've heard so much about!'

Baldmoney grinned from ear to ear. 'We *were* caught napping, Sir Herne, we were all asleep when Watervole came and woke us up!'

'Ah! a good friend is Watervole,' said Sir Herne, drawing up one long leg. 'Poor things, they've had to pack up too, I suppose?'

'Indeed they have,' said Squirrel.

'Pardon me,' said Sir Herne, noticing Squirrel for the first time, 'I don't seem to have met you before!'

'No, he came with us down the Folly last autumn, he lived in Crow Wood, you know,' said Baldmoney.

'Ah . . . How's Dodder?' asked Sir Herne, after a pause.

'Oh, he's well *and* flourishing.'

'Are you living close by?'

'Oh no, we're on our way downriver to a place Woodcock called the "Severn Sea", wherever that may be.'

'And what, may I ask, are you going to do when you get to the Severn Sea?' asked Sir Herne, looking rather surprised.

'We're going to Woodcock's island, where a hermit or a saint lies buried, and no Mortals will bother us. It's right in the middle of a grey, grey loch, so Woodcock said; Ben knows the way, Woodcock told him.'

'I expect,' said the heron, 'it's Ireland that Woodcock's talking of, he thinks a lot of the country, swears by it, says there's no place like it! I've never been there. I'm rather a home-lover, I'm afraid, England's good enough for me.'

'It's good enough for us,' said Baldmoney earnestly, 'if only the Mortals would behave themselves, but they can't. We just can't stand them, and now the Folly's gone and our tree too, we feel we must clear out and find some peace before we die!'

The heron nodded gravely. '*I* know. I can quite see your point. I, too, sometimes feel the same way myself. But you've still some way to go to reach the Severn, and when you get there I don't see how you're going to get over the Irish Sea to Woodcock's island.'

'We don't quite know ourselves yet,' confessed Baldmoney, 'but the Bens and I have a plan, and I think we might do it.'

'The *Bens*, did you say?' asked Sir Herne. 'Not Ben from Oak Tree House?'

'Yes, *the* Ben, *you* know!'

'Well I never, and where are the Bens? I haven't seen them for ages.'

'Oh, I expect they're somewhere close by, roosting in an oak or an elm. Anyway, they always show up at night when we do all our travelling.'

'So they are going too, are they?'

'Oh yes, we've decided we'll stick together, come what may. You see, we've always lived in the same tree.

Ben's ancestors did too, *you* know what it is with old friends.'

The heron nodded wistfully. He was rather a lonely old bird and had few acquaintances. Most of the Stream People were afraid of him and truth to say, he often ate a fat water-rat on the sly. And as for frogs, he fairly wolfed them down.

'Well, I wish I was coming with you,' he said after a pause. 'I do indeed. But I've got a wife and we've had a fine family this year on Poplar Island, two girls and a boy; fine children,' he said proudly.

The sun was now well down and Baldmoney realized that, without their knowing it, the evening had advanced surprisingly quickly.

The tops of the willows were no longer bathed in light and the backwater was full of green gloom and shadow. Everywhere arose the sweetly rank scent of the herbage and a bat began to hawk about overhead.

'Well,' said Baldmoney, 'goodbye, Sir Herne. We must be going. As it is, I fear we shall get in an awful row from Dodder for stopping out so late, time passes quickly with friends.'

They turned the boat about and began to paddle softly away. Baldmoney waved his cap to Sir Herne and Squirrel raised a paw.

Looking back they saw his grey form standing on the leg, his head sunk in his shoulders, and his spear couched in readiness.

'Good hunting, brother,' called Baldmoney. 'Good hunting and a good trip,' called back Sir Herne, and the next moment the clustering reeds hid him from view.

It was nearly dark when they reached the larger

backwater and saw the *Jeanie Deans* anchored against the wall of reeds. She looked indescribably cosy, her every line reflected in the still water between the lily islands. Appetizing smells were wafted from the galley stove and a dim slit of light showed through a porthole of the cabin.

They tied up the dinghy, and a minute later had scrambled aboard, hungry and tired, but feeling as though they had spent a thoroughly enjoyable evening.

CHAPTER EIGHT

At Bantley Weir

 es, those were delicious evenings and dreamy nights, as the *Jeanie Deans* progressed upon her journey.

What magic there was in simply watching the hundred shifting lights and shadows on the river. What ripple patterns, whorls and eddies, complicated geometrical designs, ever-changing, never repeating themselves!

I believe the gnomes would have liked to have spent the whole of that lovely summer pushing about like water-fowl among those secret waterways. But, after all, there was a job on hand, and if they but looked forward they could see that the time would come when the sun would cease to magic the river and those graceful beds of reeds and lush green pastures would be shrivelled and yellow under rude winter's breath.

When those days came, woe betide them should the snow and frost find them shelterless! They were gathering no harvest to see them through the cold, this idle water-gypsy experience was all very nice and soothing, but they had to finish up somewhere, somewhere that was friendly, warm, and undisturbed.

After sunset a river is as mysterious as a dense wood. The sounds one hears are echoed and magnified by the water, as from a sounding board; the plop of a rat, whistle of otter, or splash of some hefty fish, are startlingly clear.

On one of these soft luminous nights such as I have just described the *Jeanie Deans* was churning steadily along down the centre of the river. The angling season had not yet begun, otherwise it is unlikely the gnomes would have dared mid-stream. But at that late hour (it was well after midnight) not a Mortal was abroad, they had the witchery all to themselves. Dodder, as usual, was steering. Supper was over and Squirrel and the others were up on deck; it was too hot down in the cabin. Now and then the gnomes heard the quavering hoot of the Bens as they glided about the flat meadows on either side, where faint mists smoked whitely just above the tips of the mowing grass.

Occasionally one or the other wheeled over the boat, peering down at them with their big eyes.

Dodder puffed at his pipe, the tiny glow from the bowl gleaming on his nose and whiskers. He was enjoying himself. Only Dodder and Baldmoney ever steered the *Jeanie Deans*, though once, for a treat, Dodder had let Squirrel do so, when they were on their journey down the Folly from Crow Wood.

Below him, sitting up near the fo'castle, Dodder could see Sneezewort mending a rent in the back of his skin breeches. Baldmoney was busy over his notebook, drawing plans, sucking his pencil and wrinkling his forehead occasionally. Cloudberry was trying to peep over his shoulder to see what he was doing and Squirrel was up on the bridge with Dodder. After a long silence, broken only by the steady throb of the ship's screw, Dodder removed his pipe from his mouth. 'This reminds me of the night when we heard the Pan Pipes, Squirrel, d'you remember?'

Squirrel nodded and said 'Um, um.' He was watching Dodder's knotted little claws resting on the wheel. How easily their skipper steered. How *he* would like to steer, just for a minute or two! But he dare not ask Dodder. He sighed deeply.

Dodder looked at his companion. 'What's up, Squirrel? Out of sorts? Something worrying you?'

'No, nothing,' said Squirrel a trifle sadly, 'only I . . . '

'Yes, what?'

It came with a rush. 'I was only thinking how I should *love* to steer, for just a little while, just one lap.' By 'lap' Squirrel meant the full ten minutes which it took for the spring of the *Jeanie Deans* to run down, for she was driven by clockwork and not steam.

Now Dodder was in a particularly good mood that

night. The weather was calm and warm, not a breeze disturbed the silent waters, and they had made good progress lately, indeed Owl had said only that morning that in another week or two they would see the end of their journey down the river.

Like all birds, Owl was a good judge of distance and Woodcock had told him exactly how far it was to the Sea.

'Oh, well, Squirrel, I don't mind, just for a treat. And I shall be glad to take a walk along the deck.'

Squirrel was so overcome he could hardly gulp his thanks. So when the engine was re-wound Dodder handed the wheel over to him with a few cautionary remarks. 'Don't lug on it, the slightest touch is enough, she'll answer to it and—keep clear of the banks.' Squirrel nodded. His heart was beating fast with excitement. Dodder went down below to the cabin to fetch his tobacco pouch and Squirrel was at last alone, the ship was his obedient slave! How proud he felt, to think that Dodder trusted him! Trusted him with this wonderful craft! How smoothly she glided along! How sympathetic she was to every little touch on the wheel! What poetry of motion!

He glanced at the massive dark trees fringing the river, one willow branch hung right over like the arch of a bridge, and he watched it swim towards him and pass overhead, soundlessly, and on one of its graceful branches he saw two birds rolled up fast asleep. Nightingales were singing from the gardens of a riverside bungalow 'weet weet, jug, jug, pew, pew, pew!' The last beautiful sorrowful note beginning faintly and growing louder on the ear was magical.

Across the moonlit path of water he saw a vole swim busily and quickly. And Squirrel sniffed deeply, drawing his lungs full of the sweet night air. What a life, thought he, what a pity they could not go on like this always and always!

Meanwhile, Cloudberry, that restless spirit, baulked of his curiosity over Baldmoney's task, saw Dodder come down from the bridge and go into the cabin. That meant Squirrel was steering.

That wasn't fair! Dodder would never let *him* steer, so why should Squirrel? And a burning jealousy arose in his heart. He walked up the little stairs on to the bridge.

'Hullo, Squirrel, who said you could steer?'

'Dodder, of course,' said Squirrel, with a superior air. 'You don't think I'd steer without his permission do you?'

'Well, he won't let *me* steer ever,' grumbled Cloudberry. 'It isn't fair. Why should he favour you and not me?'

'Oh, don't start a quarrel, Cloudberry,' said Squirrel, wearily. 'Why must you come and upset me like this, just when I'm enjoying it so? Why can't you clear off and play Acorn Hop or something with Sneezewort?'

'He's busy, besides I don't *want* to play Acorn Hop, I want to *steer*!' Then Cloudberry bent forward and whispered, 'Come on, Squirrel, old fellow, be a sport. Dodder's below, he won't know; do let's steer for a bit, just to know what it feels like!'

'Dodder wouldn't like it,' said Squirrel. 'Besides, *I* want to steer.'

'Oh, come on, Squirrel,' wheedled Cloudberry, 'you can stand by me, and if we hear Dodder coming back you can take over right away; he'll never know! Come on, be a sport. After all, I took you for the row down the river in the dinghy, didn't I?'

'Yes, and what happened?' said Squirrel with some truth. 'We lost the *Jeanie Deans*, didn't we?'

Cloudberry relapsed into moody silence. 'What a stuffy crowd you are,' he said pettishly. 'The Heaven Hounds were far nicer to me, I wish I'd never come back.'

There was a long silence. As Squirrel continued to steer, he seemed to hear, far away, a distant murmur. Was it the night breeze in the trees and reeds? Sometimes it wasn't there at all, then it loudened.

'Wind's getting up,' said Cloudberry. 'Hark!'

'Well, what of it?' asked Squirrel. 'It's only the night wind or maybe it's a mill somewhere.'

Overhead the stars shone brightly and the moon gleamed on the spacious water meadows so that they looked like mysterious greenish plains. Sedge warblers chattered in the reeds. The wake of the *Jeanie Deans* made no more gleam than that from a rising fish, but even those minute ripples could be heard gently washing among the riverside vegetation.

Dead ahead the river took a sudden turn to the right and very dark trees hung over, the water was intensely black just there.

Cloudberry began to wheedle again. 'Come on, be a sport, Squirrel, let me take her round the bend!'

Now Squirrel was a good-natured animal. He knew if he refused Cloudberry's request he would sulk for a day after and he remembered that Cloudberry had always asked him to go with him on many little trips and excursions. It did seem a little churlish perhaps, and selfish too. So he heaved a sigh and said 'Very well then, but be careful round the bend, and if I hear Dodder coming back, I'll take over.'

Cloudberry, secretly elated at the success of his cajolings, but not thinking any more of Squirrel for acceding to his request, took over.

They went gliding round the corner in great style, but as they did so, that distant murmur, which had been trembling in the background for some little time, became suddenly insistent. 'Sounds as if another stream comes in just ahead,' said Squirrel uneasily, and then he caught sight of a glimmering white square against the background of black shadow on the bank. It was a notice-board, and peering through the gloom Squirrel could just make out three words: MIND THE WEIR.

Cloudberry had not noticed the board and Squirrel did not draw his attention to it. He suddenly felt at all costs he must regain the wheel of the *Jeanie Deans*. So he laid his hand on Cloudberry's arm and said in a matter-of-fact voice, 'Right-o, Cloudberry, I'll take the wheel now.'

'Oh no, we're not round the corner yet!'

'Yes we are. Come on, let's have it.'

'Don't be silly,' said Cloudberry, shaking him roughly off, 'my time isn't up yet. Do you hear that funny roaring noise, whatever it is?'

Squirrel was nervous now, for Cloudberry was steering far too near the right bank, close to the notice-board.

'Keep her out, it's a weir!' he cried.

'Oh goody, goody, goody,' squeaked Cloudberry. 'I'll steer right past it, and *then* you can have the wheel!'

The unfortunate Squirrel was now dancing with anxiety, and in desperation he thought of a plan.

'Quick, quick, here comes Dodder!'

But Cloudberry was too wise to be caught that way. 'Oh no, he doesn't, you're having me on—my, but doesn't that weir make a noise!'

This was too much for Squirrel. He seized hold of Cloudberry's arm and then began a silent but fierce wrestling match. Squirrel, being the larger, had an advantage and with a terrific jerk he threw Cloudberry full-length on the decking. Alas! it was too late. Though he twirled the wheel frantically, some hidden power seemed to have gripped the *Jeanie Deans*. She turned sideways to the current, but that was all. She would not answer to the helm and they were sweeping in towards that hideous precipice with gathering momentum. It was a terrible moment.

Stumbling steps came hobbling up the stairs to the bridge.

'For Pan's sake,' called Dodder, 'keep her out; or we'll be down the weir! Here!' he said savagely to Squirrel. 'Give me the wheel.'

The dull roar of waters was loudening every second, and as if under some dreadful hypnotic power, the ship and her trembling crew were swept with ever increasing velocity towards that fatal lip.

Dodder was shouting something in Squirrel's ear but now the drum of the weir was the master sound.

Faster, faster, sped the ship, until she seemed to be flying along. Her puny screws still revolved but they had no effect, and all Dodder's efforts were useless. 'We're going over!' yelled Dodder to the frightened Squirrel, but only his mouth moved, no words could be heard.

The next moment the ship tilted and slid on the very edge of the fall and then—*down* she went with a sickening speed! The thresh of foam, the roar of water, the bangs and bumps, blackness, and icy coldness, all were mixed up together as the waters closed over the boat and her helpless cargo. The time when Baldmoney and Sneezewort were carried over the mill wheel was nothing to this!

And after this sudden hell—what?

A calming, a peace, a fading sound of the fall and all four gnomes, as feeble as draggled beetles, bobbed up far downstream. Dodder, handicapped by his one leg, could not swim like the others, and had not Baldmoney grabbed him by the collar he would have gone down to join the fishes and be a feast for the crayfish.

But somehow or another they struggled to the bank and crept, like drowned mice, into the intricate tangle of the reeds. It was a battle to reach the bank beyond but they made it, half-dead.

For some moments they lay motionless, gasping and coughing, sneezing and shivering. At last Dodder lifted his head and was violently sick, for he had swallowed a lot of water.

'Ouch! Ach!' he gasped. 'Ouch! What a business!'

He looked at the others, dimly seen in the darkness among the grass. 'Are we all here? Baldmoney, you safe?'

'Ye-yes, I'm here, Dodder,' came a faint retching voice.

'Sneezewort, *you* all right?'

'A-a-all right, Dodder,' came Sneezewort's reply, between coughs and gasps.

'Cloudberry, where are you?'

'Here, Dodder!' came the gurgled reply.

'Squirrel?'

'SQUIRREL?'

'WHERE'S SQUIRREL?'

There was no response. Despite his exhaustion, Dodder somehow got to his feet. 'Squirrel, where are you?'

No answer.

'Squirrel, are you safe? Answer me!' Dodder was frantic with anxiety.

No answer, only the wind among the night trees and the now distant undertones of the weir!

CHAPTER NINE

Rumbling Mill

 tter, driven from his holt on the dying Folly, had taken up a new abode under the derelict wheelhouse of Rumbling Mill, on the main river. He and his wife were delighted with their new home. In this deeper water there were more fish to be caught and Rumbling Mill made a splendid headquarters. Indeed, as Mrs Otter said, she blessed the day they had moved, and very soon they produced a family of three cubs to celebrate the house-warming. 'Why we ever stayed up the Folly I can't think!' Mrs Otter had said to her husband. 'This river is *so* much more fun and it's better for the children!'

And in all truth Rumbling Mill *did* seem to be a 'find'. It was many years since that ponderous iron-shod wheel had revolved in the pulsing life-blood of the river, and even the Mill House itself had fallen into decay. The little plot of ground behind the house, which had once been the miller's orchard, was waist-high in nettles and wild carrot, but the twisted old apple trees, bearded with lichen and decked with mistletoe bushes, still bore red-cheecked fruit in autumn and so far was it from human ken that not even marauding boys visited it; even the stout legs of the little Shoebottom could not walk as far, for it was five miles distant from Mr Shoebottom's shop. Besides, rumour had it that Rumbling Mill was 'ha'nted'.

Old buildings when Mortals have finished with them are taken over by Nature. She rapidly gets to work, colouring the tiles, erasing the signs of cultivation, for She cultivates the ground in Her own way. Into the miller's vegetable garden She had brought masses of lovely weeds, She set the birds to work to sow wild bushes, such as elder and hawthorn, not one tiny inch of ground did She leave unplanted.

So that now, twenty years after the miller had packed up and gone, the place had reverted to a lovely wilderness which was after Nature's own heart. Blackcap and whitethroat bubbled in the undergrowth, turtle-doves purred among the willows, sedge warblers chattered and sang among the rank beds of waterside vegetation, swallows took up their abode in the tumbledown outhouses, and a pair of white barn owls took possession of the millhouse. Bats moved in and hung upside down among the dim cobwebby beams, mice and rats lived in hundreds under the old threshing floor, grass snakes lived in the orchard, wrens and tits built in the holes in the decaying brickwork, and all through the hot summer days the reed buntings sang their sleepy songs among the crowding willows by the water's edge. 'Chip, chip, chip, tetezeeo! Chip, chip, chip, tetezeeo!' they sang, never moving from the same perch day after day. Oh yes! it was a paradise for wildlings, both for plants, birds, and beasts. Standing there, waist-deep in the wild carrot, and the tall green grass of the orchard, one would never guess at half the exciting things that went on at Rumbling Mill.

You would not know, for instance, that down among the reeds a sedge warbler's nest had a cuckoo's egg in it (even the sedge warblers did not know that); you would not know of the two goldfinches' nests (one with young and the other with eggs) up in the orchard trees, nor would you hazard that there was a hawfinch's nest in the little Douglas fir close beside the millhouse. That tree, by the way, had originally been planted by the old miller after it had done duty as a Christmas tree for his children one far-off snowy wintertide. You would not know of the white owls, or the swallows and grass snakes and, least of all, would you have guessed some otters had a family under the mossy wheelhouse!

In no other part of the river would you find such a sleepy beautiful place, so green, quiet and screened by trees.

Otter was teaching his cubs to toboggan down a mud-slide hard by the tail of the old mill pool. They loved it and Otter and Mrs Otter were not above such childish delights themselves. There was no one to see but the white owls and the moon, which shone down on the roofs of the old tumbledown place. It was huge fun. But after a while Otter wearied of it and with a kick of his rudder headed upriver close to the bank. Sometimes he left the water and threaded the reed beds. Once he took to the water meadows and followed up a deep ditch which had no water in it and was overhung by stinging nettles and buttercups.

This was a short cut and besides, it was nice to leave the water for a space and travel overland. He scared several rabbits, which were hopping about in the moonlight meads and he heard a corncrake 'craking' in the mowing grass.

Otter felt very pleased with life that night. Never before had he felt so excited, so well. He was a perfect animal, at the prime of life, and sleek and powerful as a seal. He played little games with himself now and then, chasing his rudder and rolling over in the dewy grass trying to bite his shadow, until he was quite out of breath.

Not far away he could see the thick trees fringing the river, marking its course as bird-sown trees mark the course of a sunken lane.

As he ambled along, thoroughly enjoying himself, his mind turned somehow to the gnomes whom he had left far upriver with the *Jeanie Deans*. Soon they would be coming down and Otter did not want to miss his friends. It would be a sad thing if they passed Rumbling Mill without him seeing them. Besides, he was very proud of his family, and wanted to show them off, and perhaps most of all, he wanted the cubs to see the *Jeanie Deans*, for he had told them all about her.

Still, thought Otter, I can't keep hanging about every night, just on the chance of seeing them.

He suddenly realized that, what with the tobogganing and his rambling, he was very hungry. He thought of a nice fat roach or grayling and his mouth began to water. So he set off for the river. He soon found he could not be long away from it, from its music and its smells.

He pushed through a little coppice of oaks and willows until he reached a forest of dock leaves. The ground was black and oozy and a human would have sunk to his knees in it. The mire had a strong wild tang (Otter loved it) it smelt of pike and that made him more hungry than ever. He passed the skeleton of a jack, the white bones gleamed under the moon. It lay beside a moss-grown log, half-buried in the mire. It was the remains of a previous meal of his. He had not devoured it all, only a juicy back steak had been bitten out, the rats had finished the rest.

Otter was so hungry he wondered why he could ever have left it, half-eaten like that!

All at once he stopped dead. Not far off was a clump of poplars. Even though the night was so calm there was a faint rustle, almost like the sound of the sea, among the millions of leaves which made up those graceful tapering moonlit spires. And somehow, mixed up with that faint rustle, he thought he heard another sound, the sound of pipes playing, *Pan Pipes!*

Otter was very afraid. Pan's guarding arm was not always present, had not a relation of his perished in faraway Crow Wood? He shivered and the dew gleamed in pearls on his close, squat head. But when the animals hear the Pan Pipes there is no turning back; they have to obey.

So Otter went, slowly as a snail, towards the tall trees, his sleek fur creeping along his spine. As he got near the music slowly died away and Otter began to wonder if he had really heard it. There was an unreality too about the witching night; he half-expected to awake from a dream and find himself tucked up in the holt under Rumbling Mill.

And then he heard Pan's voice calling, 'Otter! Otter!' very softly.

'I am here, my Lord Pan,' said Otter, raising his muzzle. 'What is it you want of me?'

'Otter,' went on the gentle voice, seeming very close, yet far away, 'go to Bantley Weir . . . Bantley Weir. The Little People are in trouble.'

Otter, half-hidden by the dock leaves, raised himself up like a big brown weasel, his forepaws hanging against his furry stomach, his eyes searching the rustling poplars. Had he dreamt it all?

'Bantley Weir . . . the Little People . . . ' the words trailed away. There was no sound now save the very faint sweet music of the pipes coming as if from an immense distance, dying on the night wind. With a swift, almost snake-like movement, Otter turned under the docks. He went into the river as silently as a vole and rings went widening and gleaming out of the dark shadow.

He swam with great power and ease, going through the water was easier to him than going overland.

And very soon he heard, in the distance, the murmur of the weir growing louder and louder. As he swam he kept on saying to himself, 'Bantley Weir, the Little People are in trouble, Bantley Weir, hurry! Hurry! Hurry!'

Fat fish darted by, pike swirled under the lily pads, but they had no need to fear Otter at that moment. Even his hunger had vanished. One thing was in his mind: *he was wanted at Bantley Weir!*

In a very short while he reached it. He scrambled out onto a weedy block of masonry just below the great tumbling water-slide where a million flashing bubbles winked and twinked. The sound of this mass of swiftly-moving water was full of music, strange hidden notes and fairy voices, like the clamour of a vast multitude of Mortals playing and talking all at once. He looked about him. The river below the weir seemed deserted. Had he dreamt the whole thing, thought Otter again. Why had he come on this fool's errand? The moon had bewitched him. He shook himself and then took a header into the tumbled thunder at the weir's foot.

The great force of water drove him down, but Otter loved it as a skier loves the snow slopes on a mountain side. He let the current thrust and spin him, right downriver until the impetus slackened and died. And then, against the far reeds, he thought he caught sight of something show for an instant and then sink from sight. Otter dived again, his wide eyes piercing the green gloom of that underwater parlour.

A few fish darting; a sinuous snake-like root of a lily, slimy, bearded, and beset with water snails; a glimpse of a pebbly bottom, and then—there it was again!—a slow-moving form, sinking and bubbling feebly, just ahead of his nose!

It looked like the body of a drowned cat. Otter was up to it with one sweep of his rudder. It was Squirrel. Otter's squat muzzle parted as he took the body by the scruff of the neck, in the way he carried his cubs. The next moment he had broken surface and, still with the wet cold body of Squirrel held gently but firmly in his mouth, he landed on a spit of shingle, where fresh-water mussel shells, split open and left by the carrion crows, were strewn about. Gently he laid his burden down and shook his coat in the moonlight, sending out a fine silver spray.

The poor limp little object that had once been Squirrel, so fluffy and full of life, lay motionless, the water trickling and oozing out from his draggled fur onto the stones.

Yet Otter, as he looked, detected that the fur was still greasy though the white cold skin showed between the wet wisps of hair.

With his nose he pushed Squirrel over on to his stomach and began to apply artificial respiration, such as he once used upon one of his cubs which had been caught on some rusty wire on the riverbed.

Otter worked away in the moonlight, pressing with his paws on Squirrel's back. The moon sank lower behind the trees and two big owls wheeled round overhead. Otter never looked up at them, even when, with mournful cries they swooped low past him.

And then, as Otter worked and worked, he felt at last that life was flowing back. The funny little rat-like teeth gasped open once, twice; the tongue moved, the pathetic little eyes, tight closed, flickered, the eye-balls swivelled.

Otter redoubled his efforts. And in another minute or two Squirrel gave a deep gasp and opened full his eyes. He lay on his face, regarding Otter stupidly.

'It's all right, Squirrel, it's me, Otter. You're all right, I fished you out of the weir! It's no good you pretending to be an otter, old chap. You stick to the trees where I can't go. If I climbed a tree I should probably fall and break my neck. Well, it's the same with you. If you try diving and such-like games, you'll drown—see?'

Squirrel did not 'see'. Moreover he had struck his head on a stone on the river bed. He feebly moved his mouth and a little trickle of water came out of the corner. 'I'm so cold,' he whispered.

Otter took him gently by the scruff of the neck. 'You're coming along with me, my lad. I'm going to take you to Rumbling Mill. We'll be there in a brace of shakes, and I'll turn you over to my wife. If I leave you here all night you'll catch your death of cold.'

So off went Otter, carrying the now feebly-protesting Squirrel, and in next to no time he was back at Rumbling Mill.

Mrs Otter came out in an awful fuss to see what Otter had found and they carried poor Squirrel up into the cosy warm chamber in the masonry where green moss draped the door and bright hart's-tongue ferns grew from countless crannies. They bound up his head and bathed his wound. Then the little cubs all cuddled up against the cold little body, as Mr and Mrs Otter tucked Squirrel away to bed with them. And gradually the awful feeling of cold began to ebb away, minute by minute Squirrel felt the full life flooding back into his heart and every artery in his body. A beautiful glow settled on him as the otter cubs cuddled him closer still.

CHAPTER TEN

Squirrel

 n that awful moment when Dodder called aloud on Squirrel and had no reply, his heart seemed to die within him. His rage against Squirrel had been at white heat, for had not he, Dodder, left him in charge of the boat? In a measure it was his own fault, perhaps, for ever giving way like that. And it was perhaps this anger with himself that made him all the more bitter.

But now, when he realized Squirrel had gone, all his angry thoughts vanished and in their place was a dreadful desolation. We never appreciate things and persons half so much as when we are in danger of losing them. And to Dodder's own astonishment he found he had come to love Squirrel and his merry ways almost as much as he loved his brothers (he was certainly more fond of Squirrel than he was of Cloudberry).

When at last they could get their breath all four began

a systematic search along the river bank. The Bens, just when they were wanted (as always happens) were not there. They worked their way among the reeds and plants for several hundred yards but no trace of Squirrel was to be found. At last, weary and worn out, Dodder flopped down on a stone.

'It's no good looking any more,' he groaned. 'Squirrel's gone right enough, he may have struck his head on something—on the weir or even the boat, as we went over. We shan't ever see him again, our dear old fluffy Squirrel who was always so happy and full of fun!' And the tears began to well from his eyes.

The others remained silent. Sneezewort and Baldmoney were weeping too, but Cloudberry remained dry-eyed, though he looked drawn and wretched.

'It was my fault,' said Dodder, 'I should never have let him steer; it's all my fault really. I take the blame. What happened, Cloudberry? You were up on the bridge too; did Squirrel lose his head and steer too near the weir?'

Cloudberry gulped and looked at the stones at his feet. 'Yes, he seemed to lose his head entirely when he saw how close we were.'

'Why didn't you warn him?' asked Dodder. 'Surely you knew that it was silly to go so close?'

'I *did* warn him,' lied Cloudberry glibly. 'I told him to steer out more into mid-stream, but he wouldn't take any notice, it wasn't my fault.'

There was a long silence. In the east the dawn was coming up. Far away a cow began to bellow like a rich-toned foghorn; it was more of a bray than a bellow. And the gnomes could hear the distant cocks crowing one against the other.

'I can't think where the Bens can be,' said Dodder miserably. He clasped his arms about himself; all were shivering violently. Dodder did not know that whilst they were searching the reeds for Squirrel the Bens had twice passed over the weir, turning their amazed eyes this way and that as they searched for the boat.

The sun crept over the distant trees, all the birds began to sing, first one, then another, then full chorus.

The bright cheerful rays at last topped the trees and shot out warming fingers to dry those four miserable little men. Their skin jackets steamed as they sat in the sun.

While they waited there, Baldmoney caught sight of a kingfisher. It saw them, checked in mid-air and came to rest on an old mossy post below the weir. There it sat, bobbing up and down like an owl.

'This is a nice how-d'ye-do,' said he. 'Where's your boat?'

Dodder pointed to the boiling water at the weir's foot. 'She's down there,' he said grimly.

'Ah, there's thirty feet of water there, so grebe told me,' said the bird. 'She's gone for good. I met an owl downriver.'

'What, Ben you mean?'

'Yes, I believe he said his name was Ben. And I'm afraid I've got some bad news for you.'

'About our friend Squirrel?'

The kingfisher nodded and sat silent.

'Why, has Ben found him?' asked Dodder in a husky whisper.

The kingfisher nodded again.

'Dead?'

Again the kingfisher nodded. As a matter of fact, between you and me the kingfisher rather enjoyed imparting startling and appalling news.

The kingfisher looked keenly at the little men and shook his head gloomily again. 'Aye, dead, drownded, gnomes; your friend Ben saw him lying on the shingle with Otter mourning over him.'

'Otter?—Was Otter there?'

'So Ben told me,' said the kingfisher in a hollow voice.

'Did Otter find Squirrel?'

The kingfisher didn't know. 'Oh dear,' groaned poor Dodder again, 'I do wish Otter would come up here and tell us where he found him.'

Cloudberry, now he had heard Squirrel was dead, felt safer. He knew that if Dodder ever came to hear that it was he that had been the cause of the accident, then he would be eternally disgraced. For a gnome who does not own up or tell the truth is regarded as an outcast. So Cloudberry, secretly cheered, shook his head sadly and wept crocodile tears. 'Very sad, it is indeed. Squirrel was such a good sort, at times a little impetuous, perhaps, but a likeable animal. I can't think why he steered us over the weir but he always was one to think he could do things better than others.'

Dodder's eyes glittered dangerously. 'If you don't shut up, Cloudberry, I'll lay about you with my stick. Squirrel was a much better person than yourself, and I'm not so sure that you weren't the cause of the whole thing. You'd no business up on the bridge, anyway, with Squirrel. You knew my rule.' And as Dodder said this, a sudden thought struck him. He wondered it had not occurred to him before. 'I shouldn't be surprised if it *was* you who was steering when it happened . . . were you, Cloudberry?'

'Me?' asked Cloudberry in virtuous surprise. 'Of *course* not, Dodder, I wouldn't do such a thing!'

Dodder eyed him for a moment sternly and Cloudberry's gaze fell under that piercing and penetrating glance.

'Anyway,' ventured the kingfisher, 'the whole thing's over now so what does it matter? You've lost the *Jeanie Deans*, she lies in thirty feet of water, and Squirrel's drowned. Now what are you going to do?'

'Don't ask me,' said Dodder wearily. 'Come on, gnomes,' he said, turning to the others. 'We'll work our way downriver and see if we can fall in with Otter.'

'Kingfisher isn't exactly cheering, anyway,' said Baldmoney when they were out of earshot.

'Oh, don't worry about him, he's not like our old Folly King of Fishers. He was greedy and all that, but he was a good sort,' said Dodder, and they tramped on in silence.

It was evening by the time they came in sight of Rumbling Mill, another still evening, hot and quiet. When they saw the lichened roof and tall rose-red chimney poking above the willows, they went forward with caution, for all human habitations were regarded with distrust.

They had to wait awhile for dusk. They hid among the white bell nettles and Cloudberry teased the banded bumble bees as they went in and out of the flowers with their little pollen bags slung behind either thigh. Cloudberry would wait until a bumble bee had got well in the white flower and then he would hold it tightly and listen to the furious buzzings from within. When at last the prisoner was released it would go back and forth in a furious rage, and then swing away, still grumbling.

All four gnomes were in a poor way. And they were desperately hungry. They had not had any food for many hours. They sucked the white dead nettle blooms to taste the honey but it was solid food they craved. Cloudberry and Sneezewort were the most ravenous, Dodder and Baldmoney were moping over Squirrel's death.

The loss of the *Jeanie Deans* was nothing compared to the loss of their friend. Dodder went over in his mind that day in Crow Wood when they first met him. How good he was to them in his Tree Top House, giving them shelter and food . . . Behind the old mill roof the sky turned from apricot to saffron, the leaves of the orchard trees were hanging motionless, the gnats came out in thousands.

And then an interesting thing happened. Two big brown shapes appeared over the thick trees on the opposite bank and perched on the mill roof. A minute after another owl appeared from nowhere, a barn owl. And the latter attacked the intruders with great vigour. A battle royal began on the roof ridge. The hissing, snapping, and bad language was terrible. 'Why!' exclaimed Dodder, peering through some meadowsweet, 'it's the Bens!'

The fighting owls fell down the slope of the roof, clawing, scratching, and snapping their big bills, and giving vent to short half-hoots of rage. The white owl screeched like a tom-cat. All three birds flopped down into some elder bushes which grew close to the wheelhouse.

Then a dark shape came gliding out from under the mill and they saw the round neat head of Otter. He swam like a big rat into the bank and they saw him land and make off towards the combatants.

'Otter!' exclaimed Dodder. 'Come on!'

There was a dreadful scuffle going on among a bed of nettles and when all four gnomes came up they found Otter trying to make the peace. He had Mrs Ben by the leg and the white owl by the wing. Ben was sitting up in one of the apple trees shaking himself and all about them were blackbirds and finches, all chattering and calling out and making a hideous racket.

'What's all this?' said Dodder, shocked beyond measure.

Otter let go the two owls, who immediately came to grips again so that poor Otter had to wade in a second time and, heedless of scratches and nips, part the combatants once more.

The two birds subsided, panting, in the long grass, and Otter heaved a sigh. 'Oh dear, you owls, why can't you control your tempers?'

'Just you let me go,' hissed Mrs Ben, for Otter still held her by one of her legs. 'How *dare* you touch me! It's none of your business anyway.'

'Oh yes it is,' said Otter. 'All the animals and birds never quarrel at Rumbling Mill, and I'm not going to have it now.'

'They shouldn't have come on our roof,' said the white owl, 'without as much as a by-your-leave.'

'How were we to know?' said Ben from the apple tree. 'We didn't know you lived inside, how could we?'

'Now just stop wrangling,' said Otter, 'and for Pan's sake let's have some peace. The gnomes are here at last, poor things, and in a mighty poor way they must be too, after their accident. Well, well, well,' said Otter turning to greet them, 'you must be worn out and famished, welcome to Rumbling Mill,' he said heartily.

'It's good to see you, Otter,' cried Dodder. 'It's good

indeed. The first bright spot of the day. But never mind about us,' and his eyes filled with tears, 'where is poor Squirrel laid? We heard you had found him drowned.'

The Otter regarded Dodder's tearful face for a moment, and his bright little eyes flitted from one gnome to another. 'Come this way,' he said quietly. Otter proceeded a few yards through the orchard and then turned round and addressed the mill roof. 'Any more fighting and I'll come up and scrag the lot of you,' he called. But the Bens and the barn owl were nowhere to be seen; from the distant hoots and screeches the battle was going on behind the house once more. Otter, with another sigh and a shake of his head, led the way without speaking to the wheel-house.

Followed by the gnomes, he slipped with lithe ease through some old rusty railings which leant over the disused bricked-in channel and a moment later they were in a dark tunnel. Up this he conducted them and there, in a cosy little chamber at the end, the gnomes saw an unforgettable spectacle.

There was Squirrel, dear old Squirrel, with a bandage round his head, teaching the young otters how to play Acorn Hop!

Can you imagine the rush of delight which almost overcame Dodder and Baldmoney? The former stood slightly swaying for a moment and then rushed forward and threw his arms round his old friend and hugged and hugged him until he could hug no more. The young otters danced round, Mrs Otter smiled maternally, and Squirrel was crying with joy. A happy moment indeed. Rumbling Mill had not witnessed a happier one since the miller's wife had twins.

After all was over, and Dodder, feeling suddenly very weak and tired, sank down on the floor, Otter slipped away and was back within five minutes with two fat and gleaming roach wet from the mill pond.

They lit a little fire and roasted them and a happier, more jolly reunion you never saw.

CHAPTER ELEVEN

The Salvage Gang

t was not until the following evening that the gnomes could 'sit up and take notice', as the saying is. And considering the hardihood of these Little People it only goes to testify what a gruelling experience they must have been through. But after a long sleep, warmth and food, they awoke full of vitality and life and were ready for anything. Otter insisted on showing them all over Rumbling Mill. First they visited the owls up in the house top and to Dodder's relief they found that the Bens had quite made it up with the white owls and were

sharing, actually *sharing*, the same apartment with them!
Mrs Ben and Mrs White Owl (whom the former was
now calling by the affectionate name of Barny) were
apparently bosom friends, and were fussing over three
extremely ugly white woolly owlets. Ben and old Barny
had gone a-hunting together.

Then Otter conducted them through the old tumbledown threshing and milling rooms, still ankle deep in
husks and chaff (the rats had long since finished all the
grain) and they wandered about in dark underground
cellars and through mouldering outhouses; they explored
the orchard and examined with deep interest the ancient
mill stones lying one on the other with grooves cut in the
massive circular slabs.

'You've struck lucky, Otter,' said Baldmoney. 'I've
never seen such a grand place, a place after my heart:
shelter from the weather, plenty of good fishing, and as
many private apartments as you can possibly want!'

'Yes,' replied Otter, 'it's not a bad little place and
nobody ever comes near us, we haven't seen a mortal since
we moved in. They say it's haunted or something; maybe
that's the reason we're left alone.'

'And think of all those apples, Dodder!' said Baldmoney,
as he looked at the apple trees. 'What a feast in the
autumn!'

'I don't see why you want to go on downriver,' said
Otter. 'Why don't you stay here with us, the Bens, and all
of you? It seems to me to be an ideal place for us to settle
down.'

'It's an attractive suggestion, and very kind of you,'
replied Dodder, 'but I don't think we can do that. We feel
that England's no place for the Little People now. Perhaps

we might come back, say in a couple of hundred Cuckoo Years, but we've talked it all out you know and made up our minds.'

'Please yourself, of course,' said Otter, 'but I should have thought you'd have been pretty snug here. Besides, now you've lost the *Jeanie Deans*, it quite beats me how you *can* go on!'

Dodder glanced behind him at his brothers who were playing about on the mossy mill wheel and swinging like mice from the iron bars. 'The fact is, Otter, I wanted a quiet talk with you about her.'

'Come this way then, Dodder,' said Otter, nodding. '*They* seem to be amusing themselves and Squirrel's still tucked up with the cubs. I know the very place for a quiet talk, follow me.'

He pushed through a bed of dead nettle and led the way into a dense reed jungle where a mouldering punt lay completely screened by rank vegetation.

'Nobody will disturb us here,' said the hospitable animal, climbing into the punt. 'Sit down on the seat there and you can talk as long as you like. I often sneak off here for a quiet nap.'

'Well!' began Dodder, drawing out his pipe and filling it. 'I wanted to know whether you could give me some advice. The ship's foundered good and proper, and a kingfisher told us she lies in thirty feet of water under the weir.'

Otter nodded. 'Yes, there's all that just under the weir, what of it?'

'Well,' Dodder hesitated shyly, 'I . . . I wondered very much, Otter, whether you could go down and have a look at her, see if she's damaged and what you think about our chances of salvage.'

Otter whistled. 'Salvage! Can't see how we can do that, I couldn't move her by myself.'

'No,' said Dodder, 'I don't expect you could, but I wondered whether you and I could talk out a plan and see if there's not some way of getting her up.'

Otter sat on the bottom boards of the punt and twitched his whiskers, a habit of his when he was thinking deeply.

'It *might* be done,' he said at last, 'though it will be a big job. But before we talk about that, how about me going down and seeing what she looks like, eh?'

'Oh will you, Otter?' cried Dodder gleefully, clapping his friend on the shoulder. 'What a grand fellow you are! I knew you'd help us if you possibly could.'

So they got out of the punt and made their way along the riverbank towards Bantley Weir. Very soon Rumbling Mill was left behind and Otter, coming to a shingle spit, whispered to Dodder to climb on his back.

'Hold on tightly,' he said, 'I'll go slowly.'

It was a precarious perch for the one-legged Dodder but he plucked and twisted a bunch of rushes and put it under Otter's chin, like a pair of reins, and the next moment they were out from the bank.

The cold water rippled along Dodder's left knee but he enjoyed the novel ride; Otter swam so steadily and smoothly, threading his way with great skill through sedges and willow bushes which, in places, grew out from the bank.

Before very long Dodder could hear the low voice of Bantley Weir coming to them across an arm of the river and soon he saw the mass of trees and the silvery white slope of the falling water.

Otter landed on the bank just below and together they went over the stones along the water's edge. After days of drought the sky was overcast and a fine rain was falling which seemed to bring out the scents of meadow and undergrowth.

Dodder showed Otter as best he could where the *Jeanie Deans* had taken her final plunge and then, with a shake of his muzzle, Otter swam off. Dodder could see his small head forging up on the left of the fall. Then he saw him dive.

Otter went down into the underwater gloom. All about him the currents swayed and pushed him, but by nice adjustment he kept his body 'trim' and as he swam deeper the gloom deepened. Tiny silver bubbles, like beads of quicksilver, netted his smooth short hairs. He swam over a shelf of ragged concrete and a large barbel darted from under the overhanging edge. Otter glimpsed the curious hanging appendages at each corner of its mouth.

Normally that barbel would have been easy meat but he let it go. He knew every inch of Bantley Weir and had caught many a fat fish there among the broken smother of the falls. Millions of bubbles, like champagne bubbles, bored down past him, streaming and tickling along his sleek sides.

He turned along the weir foot, searching among massive blocks of masonry and large stones. A bright tin lid glittered in the gloom and Otter turned it over with one scoop of his paw and passed on, hunting as carefully as an eel.

A blackened stump of a tree he found, with a wire pike trace, complete with float, caught in it. The float was streaming out on the line with the bore of the current but he saw no sign of the wreck. Moreover he had to come up for air so he twirled sideways and let himself drift and rise. When he broke surface he was well below the shingle where he had left Dodder and the latter had his back to him. He was crouching behind a stone watching the weir foot expectantly, his long ears pricked. Otter smiled to himself. Poor old Dodder, he must find the *Jeanie Deans* for him, if it took him all night.

He ran along the shore and shook himself and Dodder, startled, turned to meet him. 'Goodness! you gave me a scare! Well, Otter . . . any sign of her?'

Otter shook his head. 'Not yet, Dodder, but I'll find her.'

It was raining heavily now, the drops raising little thorns all over the surface of the weir pool. Everywhere the thirsty earth was drinking deeply and a faint mist lay on the river which smoked upwards, but Dodder ignored the wet.

Otter dived again. This time he searched the river bed some yards below the weir foot. It was not so deep there, the shingle sloped gradually upwards and the race of the current seemed more pronounced. A few cushions of water weed and poa grass streamed out black and waving, like the tentacles of an octopus, and from under them a banded perch with spines erect darted in a swirl of sand. This time Otter could not resist a natural impulse. He headed the fish into an angle between a large stone and an old petrol can and caught it deftly.

With the fish in his mouth he turned again and then—he saw the *Jeanie Deans*! She lay on her side with her foremast jammed under a rock, and there was a big dent on one side of the funnel. As Otter swam past and over her he saw a squat ugly little fish with a spotted back squirm into the cabin door, a bull head.

With the fish still in his mouth Otter turned again and bobbed up abreast of Dodder but in mid-river. He swam across to him and laid the perch on the shingle where it gasped once and lay still, though its red fins quivered slightly. 'I've found her, Dodder, she's lying in about ten feet of water, just out there, the force of the current must have washed her down.'

'Is she badly knocked about?' asked Dodder anxiously, hardly glancing at Otter's fine catch.

'Funnel's a bit dented, but I don't think she's holed; let's go back to Rumbling Mill and we'll talk it over!'

Dodder grasped the perch by the gills and they set off for home.

It was raining really hard when they got back to the Mill and Dodder was glad to be out of it. It came down steadily, in warm hissing rods, which blurred the mill pool's surface and came spouting off the old mill roof in rattling silver threads. He found Baldmoney and the rest all grouped round a fire in the old malt house. The young otters were there too. It was the first time they had seen a fire and they were held by it. All, including Squirrel, whom Mrs Otter had tucked up in a sacking shawl, were sitting in a circle listening to Cloudberry. He was in his element, for there was nothing he liked better than showing off, and he thought himself no end of a hero. It was *I* this, and *I* that, and how he had gone all the way to Spitzbergen with the Heaven Hounds.

But on the appearance of Dodder and Otter he looked self-conscious and foolish. His voice trailed away into a thin squeak and it was quite laughable to see him slowly deflating like a toy balloon.

The truth was, he was afraid of Dodder, and he was afraid also that Squirrel would let out how the accident had happened. He had even begged Squirrel not to say a word and the latter animal was very offended. Just as if he would!

Dodder had never once referred to the accident though it was obvious that he thought that Squirrel was to blame.

Cloudberry tried to whistle a jaunty tune when he saw Dodder and Otter, and when the former gave him a withering look of contempt he took himself off for a walk in the pouring rain. As he went along he muttered away to himself and then, quite suddenly, he realized how he hated Dodder. The more he thought of him the greater grew his hatred. If ever the true facts of the accident came out, as well they might, then he knew he would be disgraced forever. If only he could find some way of getting rid of Dodder! It was an ugly thought and at first he put it away but it returned like a black and hideous imp whispering on his shoulder, 'Why not get rid of him?' There would be no more snubs, no more being 'put in his place'. Sneezewort didn't count, and Baldmoney was easily handled; he was a good-natured gnome, always busy with his own plans. He, Cloudberry, would become the skipper of the band, he could bend everyone to his will, he would be master of the expedition. So on he stumped up the river bank, all alone in the wind and rain, his hands behind his back, thinking these ugly thoughts. Dodder had only one leg. It would be easy! A knock on the head when no one was looking, a push, and Dodder would sink like Squirrel had sunk, and nobody would be any the wiser!

Meanwhile, back in Rumbling Mill, the fire was burning brightly and all the animals and gnomes crowded round it. 'Let's send for the Bens!' exclaimed Dodder. 'They ought to be here, for we've got to have a meeting, a very important meeting.'

'Better ask the Barnies too,' said tactful Otter, 'we can't leave them out of it, especially as they are now so pally with the Bens.'

So Sneezewort was sent upstairs to find them and very soon everybody was present and Dodder got to his feet.

'Well, souls all,' he began, 'first of all I want to say something about the welcome we've had here. We won't ever be able to repay Otter for all his kindness, and it's very nice of you all to make us so at home at Rumbling Mill. And now we're here, I've something to say to you.'

'Cloudberry isn't here,' interrupted Sneezewort from the shadows, 'he went out some time ago.'

'Never mind Cloudberry,' said Dodder impatiently, 'we can't wait for him. I'm afraid he is a very different gnome since he went away with the Heaven Hounds, he seems to have changed a lot. But never mind that. What I have to say is this: Otter and I have just been up to Bantley Weir, where as you know, we had the misfortune to lose the *Jeanie Deans*. The blame of the accident rests on my shoulders and I feel I ought to explain how it happened. Against my judgement I let Squirrel here steer the ship and owing to his inexperience he steered too close to the weir. It was just bad luck that I should have chosen that moment to go below. But that's all over and done with. What I have to tell you is this. Otter and I have been up to the weir and Otter very kindly dived for us. He's found the wreck!'

'Found it!' exclaimed Baldmoney. 'Can we get her up?'

'Not so fast, Baldmoney,' said Dodder. 'I'm coming to that. I've called this meeting to discuss the possibility of raising her.'

'Impossible,' said Ben, 'you'll never salvage her.'

'One moment,' said Dodder. 'Otter found her lying, not right under the weir, but in shallower water below it. Evidently the current had washed her there. She lies in not more than ten feet of water. Now, what we've got to do is to find some way of raising her and I want suggestions.'

'I'll make a diving suit,' said Baldmoney at once. 'I'm sure I could.'

'*Do* be practical, Baldmoney, *please*,' said Dodder. 'You can't possibly do that, clever as you are, and if you did, we shouldn't be any nearer to the solving of the difficulty.'

'Let's get Grebe to dive,' suggested Sneezewort, 'he spends most of his life on the river bed.'

'That won't help either,' said Baldmoney. 'He couldn't do any more than I could. Otter's the most likely.'

Otter, who had been sitting very quiet twitching his whiskers and staring into the fire, spoke up. 'I have an Idea, Dodder, if you'll let me speak. I can't raise her by myself, but if I get some of my relations we might do it!'

There was a pause and the young otters began to jump about in excitement for they were longing to see the famous ship. Mrs Otter had to 'shush' them to silence before Otter could continue.

'My idea is,' he said, 'that we send word to them; I have many relations farther downriver and we'll ask them to come up here and help. At a pinch we can muster seven or eight of them. With our combined efforts I believe we could get her up!'

'A splendid idea!' exclaimed Dodder, clapping his hands, and everyone nodded approval.

'Then it shall be done,' said Otter, after the hubbub had died down. 'We'll send word to them tomorrow by kingfisher, vole, and moorhen.'

'Ben and I will tell them too,' said Mrs Ben.

'Why wait?' put in Barny. 'I'll be off now, if you like. I know where every otter in the river has his holt and now's the time to catch 'em.'

'Very well then,' said Otter. 'You and the Bens can go off right away. Are you sure you know where they live? Willow Holt, Gravelly Reach, Heronbanks?'

'I know,' said Barny impatiently. 'I know them all.'

'Right, then off you go!' exclaimed Otter. 'And tell them we want them up here tomorrow evening at last light!'

CHAPTER TWELVE

Cloudberry Takes a Walk

 loudberry, his black thoughts in accord with the black night, tramped on. After a while the rain ceased and the stars came out, but he was in such an ugly frame of mind the beauty of the fresh moist fields were quite wasted on him. The more he thought of Dodder, the more he wanted to dispose of him. Once Dodder was out of the way he could do exactly as he liked. He'd make them all go round the world, but Squirrel they would leave behind, the silly creature. He couldn't think what his brothers were about, joining up with him in the first place. In fact, why shouldn't he 'bump off' Squirrel too, dead animals tell no tales!

He left the riverside and made his way to a wild common where gorse bushes, clumps of thicket, elder, thorn, and bramble formed a tangled wilderness. Bub'ms (rabbits) were everywhere, bobbing their white scuts, and several pairs of nightingales were singing lustily. But their song held no beauty for Cloudberry in his present mood, he wanted complete quiet for the hatching of his hideous plans. He sat down under a furze bush and bit his long black nails. The thought of the jolly gathering at Rumbling Mill only made him all the more bitter.

As he sat there, his eyes wandered among the tangled grass and brambles. Soon he spied two fine edible fungus with their chestnut brown domes gleaming in the shadow. He plucked them and took out his knife to peel off the skin. Gnomes regard these fungi as a great delicacy, much as we prize truffles.

But all of a sudden he put his knife back in his belt. No, he had a grand idea! He knew how fond Squirrel was of edible fungi. Many times he had seen the squirrels in the woods eating them and had found the brown caps with a piece bitten out of them, much as a piece is bitten out of an apple.

Cloudberry knew that were other fungi, wicked poisonous fungi, and some had quite a nice taste. Why not find some Fly Agaric or, better still, Death Cap, that innocent-looking white toadstool which grew in waste places? He could mix them in with the edible fungi and make an appetizing brew! The gnomes were always bringing back mushrooms and other edible fungi for the pot. He could poison off the lot, not only Dodder and

Squirrel, but the others too, and he would then have the great distinction of being *the last gnome in the whole of Britain*! What a fuss everybody would make of him then! The last gnome! He was so pleased with himself he skipped about with glee. No need to knock anyone on the head; just mix a few Agarics in with the rest and the deed would be done! It would be an easy matter to pretend to eat some himself. In fact, he could fill their five little porringers (made out of chestnut cups) himself, of course taking care not to put any poison in his own. Cloudberry rubbed his hands together and danced for joy. The next thing was to find some Death Caps or Fly Agaric. The latter is a bright scarlet fungus, spotted with leprous white, a strangely fascinating, yet dreadful growth. He put the two edible fungi in his skin cap and set off into the furze. Not far away was quite a little wood. A likely place!

It was a difficult matter threading his way through this tangled place but at last he found a rabbit run and this he followed. He had not gone down this very far when he heard the alarm note of a nightingale: 'Ueeee Pew! Ueeee Pew!' Interested, he turned aside, and after pushing about for some time, he came to a mass of privet, white in flower, which made the night air heavy with its strange scent.

Beneath it grew ivy, an ideal place for a nightingale's nest. The parent birds were flying round in a terrible state. 'Oh dear, my babies! My poor babies!' the mother kept wailing. 'Save them! Save them! Help! Help!'

Cloudberry stood watching them for some time and then called out, 'What's the matter, what's all the fuss about?' and then he felt a cold little fear. Stoats liked baby birds. If it was a stoat he would make a hasty retreat.

'Help! Help!' called the mother nightingale again. 'The Worm of Death has found my babies!'

Cloudberry, who had been poised for instant flight, took heart. 'Where is your nest?' he asked.

'Under the privet!' wailed the poor distracted birds. 'Save them! Save them!'

He pushed his way very cautiously through the bushes, treading with the utmost care. Under the ground ivy he heard a faint rasping rustle which sent the hair creeping in his beard. He peered closer and suddenly saw, with quite a start, the squat and tapered body of an adder. It was silver grey in colour, exactly matching the grey lichen which grew on the mouldering tree branches which lay about on the ground. He saw its coils smoothly contracting as it gulped down the last of the nightingale babies.

He could not suppress a shudder. The gnomes had no quarrel with the snakes, nor they with them. The timid grass snakes were their friends and, for that matter, the sinister adders were too. But there was one thing about the adders: they had a disconcerting habit of biting you if you trod upon them or stumbled on them unawares. So Cloudberry stood where he was and called softly:

'Worm of Death! Worm of Death! Are you there?'

'Yessssss!' came the low hissing response. 'I am here, who callsssss?'

'It's me, Cloudberry!'

There was a silence and then the ivy leaves began to move and rustle and he saw the evil head, with its fat poison glands bulging behind each cheek and the glittering eyes which he dare not meet with his own.

'I hope you have dined well and had good hunting,' said Cloudberry faintly.

'Yesssss! I have had good hunting, gnome! Yessssss! Mossssst satisssssssfactory! But what bringsssss you here?'

'We're staying at Rumbling Mill,' said Cloudberry.

'Rumbling Mill! A fassssssinating placcccce!'

'Indeed it is,' said Cloudberry. 'We're on our way downriver but we lost our boat by Bantley Weir so we're staying on with Otter for a bit.'

'Do the white owlsssssss ssssstill live up in the mill housssse?' asked the adder. Cloudberry noticed a distinct bulge in the middle of its black-patterned body and he shuddered again.

'Yes indeed, and they have a nest up in the loft.'

'And have they any nicccccce fat youngssssssters?' said the adder, coming out a little farther from the ivy.

'Yes, they have,' said Cloudberry and then wished he had kept silent.

'Ah,' said the adder, 'ssssstill in down I ssssssuppose?'

'Yes, they are,' said Cloudberry. 'Why?'

'I wassss jusssst enquiring, I do not like the white owlsss but I like baby owletsss, very much, yessssss, very muchshsh, they are asss good asss nightingalessssss, though they do not ssssing sssso sssweetly!'

Cloudberry found he was trembling.

Meanwhile the poor nightingales, beside themselves with grief, wailed above their heads.

'What bringssssss you to my pressservesss, gnome?' asked the adder after a pause.

'I was just taking a stroll,' said Cloudberry, beginning to regret he had come and wishing he was back at Rumbling Mill.

'It'sss a good thing you did not ssstep on me in the dark,' said the adder, 'I sssssometimes make misstakes! I like to be warned when gnomes are tressspasssssssing!'

'I'm sorry, Worm of Death, I didn't know you lived here.'

'Didn't Otter tell you I wassss here?' asked the snake.

'No, he didn't; he never warned us.'

'Then he sshould have done. It ssssshowsss lack of ressssspect.'

'He's been so busy,' said Cloudberry, hopping from one leg to the other.

'What are you carrying in your hat?' asked the snake.

'Edible Fungi, for our supper.'

'You eat that sssstuff?' said the adder. 'You sssurprisse me!'

'Oh yes, we think it a great delicacy,' said Cloudberry, 'but we do not eat the Death Cap or the Fly Agaric.'

The adder hissed gently. 'Ah, I know them, they grow not far from here, clossse to my housse, I like the sssmell of them. Yesssss! but you are welcome to them if you wisssssh!' and the adder gave a squirm of mirth at its own joke. 'Come, I will sssssshow you my housssse!'

'Oh,' said Cloudberry, 'if you don't mind, Worm of Death, I won't come just now, I must get back.'

'Oh yesssssss you will, you musssssst sssssee my housse, I'll sssssshow you the way.'

Cloudberry was trying very hard not to appear frightened and he did not want to offend the adder so what could he do but follow? And after all, he thought, it might be useful to know where the Agarics grew, *quite* useful.

So he followed the adder through the furze. It moved sluggishly because it was full fed. It was also sleepy.

'I musssst sssshow you where I live,' it hissed over its shoulder, 'becausssse you might ssstep on me in the dark sssometime and that would be dissssasssstrousssss for all of usssss!' and the little eyes burned more brightly than ever.

Adder led the way under some dark trees to a low ivy-grown bank. Far behind, Cloudberry could still hear the wailing of the poor nightingales. He felt he was in a very evil place.

After gliding along the foot of the bank a little way the adder came to a small hole, which looked not unlike a mole-hole. Cloudberry was half afraid that the adder would press him to follow it inside but it was drowsy and wanted to sleep off its supper.

'Thisssss issss my houssssse,' said the adder, turning round and regarding him. 'I would assssk you in but I want to ressst. But I'll be sssseeing you again!' it hissed and then, inch by inch, it vanished into the hole. Cloudberry saw the black-patterned tapered body like a nightmarish worm slowly sucking in and then he was alone. A great relief passed over him. He'll be seeing me, will he? thought Cloudberry. Not if I know it!

Clutching his hat he turned to go and then he remembered what the adder had said about the Agarics.

'Close to his home', he had said. He followed the bank along a short distance, treading gingerly and gazing about him. Adder's remark about 'minding his step' obsessed him. He felt like a man walking through a minefield.

And then, at the foot of the bank under some yews, he saw a clump of glimmering red toadstools. They were the Agarics sure enough. Quickly he gathered them and put them in his hat. And then, suddenly afraid, he turned and ran as fast as he could out of that dark and forbidding place.

When at last he reached Rumbling Mill he hid the poisonous fungi in the hollow of a willow hard by the wheel house. They would do for supper the following night, and meanwhile he had to lay his plans.

CHAPTER THIRTEEN

The Raising of the Jeanie Deans

he following evening there was great
excitement at Rumbling Mill. As soon as it
got dark the other otters began to arrive.
Dodder and Otter counted them as they
came in. Evidently the Bens and Barny had
done their job well.

Baldmoney suggested that they should all have a feast
before they went to business, but Dodder said nobody
could work on a full stomach. 'Let's have a feed when
we've raised the ship,' he said. 'Sneezewort can stay and
get it ready.'

'I wanted to see the *Jeanie Deans* brought up,' grumbled
Sneezewort. 'I always have to cook and do all the dirty
work. It isn't fair.'

'Let's toss up who's to stay then,' said Dodder. 'That's
the fairest way.'

Cloudberry, who had been listening, suddenly saw that
now was his chance; it was as though it had all been
planned. It couldn't have worked out better! 'Don't

worry,' he said. 'I'll stay and cook the supper. I don't mind, you leave it all to me.'

This was so unlike Cloudberry, Dodder was amazed. What had come over him? It was astonishing.

'Well, I call that pretty decent of you, Cloudberry,' said Dodder. 'We'll make it up to you somehow.'

'And perhaps you wouldn't mind keeping an eye on my babies,' said Mrs Barny. 'They're as good as gold. I've given them their supper and if you can just look in once or twice to see if they want anything, I'd be obliged.'

'Certainly, ma'am, I'll be delighted,' said Cloudberry. 'What time will you be back, Otter?'

'There's no knowing,' said Otter. 'It may take half the night, if she's jammed tight in the river bed. Expect us when you see us.'

And with a wave of a paw he turned upriver and everybody followed behind. Baldmoney carried a strong rope made out of twisted grass, Sneezewort carried a loop of wire they had found in the malt house, and Dodder had a large six-inch nail over his shoulder, which might come in useful as a crowbar. Cloudberry stood by the wheel house and watched the little party out of sight round the bend of the river. The moon would be rising late, the first part of the night would be dark. He sat down on the grass and watched the water. The rain had gone and it looked as though the hot weather was coming back. The night was utterly still. Already the stars were beginning to wink and blink and the sound of the river seemed very loud.

When should he prepare his hideous Devil's brew? Should he wait awhile until it was quite dark? Where had Sneezewort put the porringers? In a minute or two he would have a look. His heart beat fast. Rumbling Mill seemed suddenly very hostile and watchful. It was quite eerie to think he was all alone with only the young otters in their holt under the wheel house and the baby Barnies up in the loft. The youngsters had been told to be good children because their parents were going out and they had also been told that 'Uncle Cloudberry' would come and see if they were all right.

Cloudberry could not help smiling to himself at the role of nursemaid assigned to him. For a long while he sat on the stones by the wheel house watching the bats flickering above him, hardly visible. Now and then they would suddenly dive close to the surface of the river and chase each other about with tiny mouse-like squeaks.

The trees about the mill grew very black, as did the water under them. He smelt the almost overpowering smell of river water and slimy weed. A fish splashed out in the mill pool. Otter had said that Rumbling Mill was haunted. Haunted by what? Cloudberry shivered. It was horrid being all alone like this. He stole under the wheel house and listened. The baby otters were sleeping soundly. He had better see if the baby Barnies were all right too. He wasn't taking any chances, he didn't want a soul to see him fetch the fungi.

He stole into the door of the mill house and started to climb the rickety stairs. Rats scuttled about in the darkness and made him very jumpy. The old house was full of clicks and rustlings and quiet subdued footfalls. How dark it was in here! But gnomes can see well in the dark; to a Mortal it would have been utter blackness.

Hist! What was that? He thought he heard Dodder's halting tread on the stair! No . . . only his guilty conscience. He must pull himself together. He would see if the Barnies wanted anything, then he would go and fetch the fungi from the hollow tree and prepare his ghastly brew. By this time tomorrow night he would be the last gnome in Britain, what glory would be his! He went on up the stairs. Soon he found himself in the loft.

Cobwebs hung from the beams, draped like grey rags from rafter to rafter. Through a large gap in the roof a star was winking down at him and up in one corner under the tiles he could see a smudge of white, which was the woolly bodies of the baby Barnies. They seemed to be wide awake, snapping their bills at him in quite a friendly way.

Cloudberry tiptoed back to the stair head. Once again he thought he heard Dodder's halting step below, but it was only his imagination. Now he would go and prepare his deadly brew which would rid him of all his troubles and bring him such glory. He stopped again. The well of the staircase seemed like a pit. He thought he heard a faint rustling below, like autumn leaves. A rat perhaps? Cloudberry, suddenly filled with a strong desire to get out of the mill into the open air, started to scurry down the stairs like a scared mouse.

Meanwhile Bantley Weir was the scene of feverish activity and excitement. Never before had so many otters been gathered at that spot. And somehow or another many of the River Folk had got wind of what was happening and the shores on either side were thick with water voles and water birds. Grebe was there, yes even aristocratic grebe! And he offered to dive with the otters and help put the wire hauser under her. Otter led off, followed by his relations, and they dived down, one after the other, like a school of porpoises. Dodder, Baldmoney, and Sneezewort, together with the Bens, stood about on the shingle watching the dim water below the weir. Now and again they saw a round head bob up for air and then down it would go again.

Otter led his band to the wreck unerringly. She lay as he had last seen her and the first job was to free the mast from under the stone. It took three of the otters working together to do it. Then the wire was pushed under the hull. This was a more difficult matter and took some time, necessitating several trips to the surface for air. But at last the task was done, the wire was passed under the hull and pulled tight by strong teeth (this had of course been Baldmoney's idea!).

Then with three otters at the stern and three at the bow and Otter and a companion hanging on to the wire, they began to pull her towards the shore. Though she was a heavy ship she moved much more easily than was to be expected, and it may be that there was still some air in her bulkheads.

In any case, after about an hour's hard work, a cheer went up as the delighted crowds saw the mast of the *Jeanie Deans* once more appear above the surface of the river. It was a more difficult matter when they got the ship into the shallow water and the otters had to work very hard with frequent pauses for breath. And then at last, not a couple of hours after the operations had started, the ship was high and dry on the shingle! All hands set to work. She was tipped on her side and all the water drained from her hull and when this was done Baldmoney and Squirrel went below to see what damage had been done, while the tired and exhausted otters took 'an easy' on the shingle.

Of course it was only to be expected that the interior of the ship had suffered a good deal. The cabin was in an awful state. But the sopping skin rugs and coats were spread out to dry on the stones and with the help of Dodder and the owls, it was not very long before the *Jeanie Deans* was looking quite presentable once more.

While the others attended to the interior of the cabin, Baldmoney got to work on the engine. It was red with rust and at first it looked as though she would never be able to voyage again. But by scraping away with his knife he got rid of most of it, and when they tried the key they found she was all in order.

Dodder was delighted, indeed he was so overcome with gratitude to the otters, he could hardly find words to thank them. At last the time arrived to start her up and take her downriver. Squirrel, Baldmoney, and Sneezewort went aboard, and with a grand flotilla as escort—a flotilla composed of grebes, water voles, otters, and the owls, she at last moved off under her own power on her way to Rumbling Mill.

It seemed a miracle that everything should have gone so well! As Dodder said to Baldmoney, 'What we want now is a nice hot day tomorrow to dry her out. The bunks won't be fit to sleep in for some time but she isn't damaged much.'

'And I'll soon get the dent out of the funnel,' said Baldmoney, looking up at it as he stood by Dodder's side, 'and the foremast's broken too. We shall have to fit another, we must have a smart ship.'

Dodder sighed a happy sigh. He was once again at the wheel of his beloved *Jeanie Deans*, everything was all right with the world.

At last they saw Rumbling Mill in the distance and very soon, on a word from Dodder, the engine was shut off and the good ship came gliding gently in to her anchorage under the wheel house. They tied her up securely and then, thanking the otters, who were dropping off downriver one by one, Dodder came ashore, followed by Squirrel, Baldmoney, and Sneezewort.

'Now for some supper,' said Baldmoney, rubbing his hands. 'A good job done, if you ask me. I wonder what Cloudberry has got for us, I feel as though I could eat anything!'

'And so do I,' said Dodder heartily, mopping his forehead, for it was a hot night and the work had been hard.

But when they peeped into Otter's house, where they always had their meals, all was in darkness. The young Otter cubs were sleeping peacefully, but there was no sign of a fire or of any supper laid. Mystified, Dodder and the others searched the mill from top to bottom.

Cloudberry had completely vanished!

'I can't make him out at all,' said Dodder. 'He said he'd have supper for us when we came back, what *can* he be doing?'

'Perhaps he didn't expect us back so soon,' said Sneezewort.

'P'raps he's gone fishing,' said Otter.

Up in the loft the young owlets were safe and sound. They said that 'Uncle Cloudberry' had come to see if they were all right about an hour after the others had left. It was all very, very mysterious! At any rate they did not let this little mystery spoil their triumph. Everyone turned to and prepared supper and it didn't take long for Otter to bring in some nice fresh perch. And as to Squirrel, there was plenty for him. The store of nuts in the hold of the *Jeanie Deans* had not suffered in any way, and everyone voted that the night's work had gone without a single hitch.

But what had happened to Cloudberry?

If he had had his way, the happy party now sitting down to a jolly supper would be partaking of his poison, and the dawn of a new day would have found him the master of the *Jeanie Deans* and with the distinctive title of the Last Gnome in Britain!

But Pan had willed it otherwise. It was Pan who whispered into the ear of the Worm of Death away on Bantley Heath that three white owlets in down would make him a fine supper. It was Pan who guided those sinister coils to Rumbling Mill and it was he who cleverly arranged that the panic-stricken Cloudberry, his guilty mind full of his own dreadful project, should elect at that moment to come tumbling down the mill-house stairs! As the Worm of Death had warned Cloudberry, it was wise to tread carefully when adders were about.

And so it was, that as the Worm of Death ascended the dark stairway, with his mind full of what a nice meal those three owlets would make, Cloudberry planted one foot on the squat and banded body. The Worm of Death struck right, struck left, and his wicked teeth went home. Rat, lizard, owlet, or gnome, they were all the same to the Worm of Death. He made his leisurely meal and departed. He would save up the young owlets for another day.

CHAPTER FOURTEEN

Holidays

hen, on the following morning, there was still no sign of Cloudberry, the mystery deepened. But I cannot say that anybody bothered their heads very much. Dodder ventured the opinion that he had gone off on another of his lonely travels and that their absence from the mill that night had given him the opportunity to slip away. And as time went by and still there was no sign or clue, this explanation was more or less accepted. Then Sneezewort, returning from a fishing expedition from the direction of Bantley Weir, found Cloudberry's belt and knife on the edge of the river. The Worm of Death, finding this indigestible, had got rid of it as he made his way back to Bantley Heath.

'He must have fallen into the river somehow and drowned himself,' said Dodder. 'Either that, or he dropped the knife as he went off on another of his voyages of exploration, in which case we can't go and look for him again.'

Squirrel, poking about by the millhouse, also discovered the collection of fungi, but there was nothing to suggest any connection with Cloudberry.

A chance remark by Dodder brought to light the truth about the loss of the *Jeanie Deans* and after learning Squirrel's story, the disappearance of their evil-minded brother was not referred to again. It was all very sad. Cloudberry had once been a good gnome, but his roving life had changed him entirely. But there were much more important things to think about than the disappearance of the ne'er-do-well.

The *Jeanie Deans* had to be made shipshape again and there was much work to be done, both on her and in her. Luckily the weather was hot, which was just what the gnomes wanted. Baldmoney spent two whole days hammering the dent out of the funnel—a tedious, noisy, and warm business.

Sneezewort and Dodder got to work on the inside of the cabin, polishing the woodwork and scrubbing the bunks; there was not much time to enjoy those glorious summer days and nights.

But in their idle moments they would slip away to fish or ramble along the riverside, and sometimes, when the weather was excessively hot, Baldmoney and Sneezewort went for swims with Otter. He knew every mile of the river about Rumbling Mill and what games they had, rolling naked about among the buttercups, or playing hide-and-seek among the bullrushes and reed mace!

It was astonishing how quickly the young Barnies grew up. It was not long before they were out of the nest and sitting in a row along the roof ridge, like so many hideous gargoyles, hissing to be fed.

The baby otters were now out and about too and sometimes Otter would take them all, gnomes included, to toboggan on the mud slides. This was a great treat and Baldmoney and Sneezewort loved it. Never before had they had so much swimming and Otter said that if they stuck at it they would soon swim as well as he did. He even taught them how to hunt fish. This was great fun. In the evenings, after the heat of the day, the cubs, Baldmoney and Sneezewort and Otter would go off to some favourite hunting ground of his and there he would set some fat roach or perch 'on fin' and the hunt would be up. They worked with considerable technique. Otter would 'head' the fish and the gnomes would help him corner it under the bank or against a stone. At those times, Dodder, being barred from such sports by his disability, would go off alone and hunt up his many friends.

He enjoyed those rambles by the lush river banks, looking up the various families which were just beginning to find their legs and wings. Once he saw a cuckoo perched on a fence post 'birds-nesting'. When a cuckoo wants to find a nest in which to lay its eggs it just sits still in some likely spot for hours on end, watching the other birds. This was a dodge which the gnomes themselves practised and it is one of the most productive ways of finding birds' nests and saves much needless effort and painful scratches.

This cuckoo on the post missed nothing. She saw the tree pipit soaring over his singing tree on the edge of a cornfield and after a while she saw him go down among the green grass on the headland where his mate was sitting. And the cuckoo watched a pair of sedge warblers building in some sweet briar close to the river, and the reed warblers likewise, busy among the tall bullrushes' stems, and made up her mind where she would lay her eggs. The reeds in which the reed warblers built were the real bullrushes, which have no brown woolly heads like pokers (the latter are the reed mace). The true bullrush has a feathery graceful flower head. As the cuckoo sat in the sun she wagged her spotted tail from side to side like a pleased dog. Dodder had never seen that happen before.

And everywhere the fields, woods, and copses were full of baby things just out of the nest: thrushes, blackbirds, moorhens, dabchicks, blackcaps, whitethroats, garden warblers, and finches. Their varied squeaks for food were insistent.

Dodder was able to save many a little life. He found a baby song thrush which had fallen into the river. He fished it out and sat it in the sun until it had dried and then gave the mother thrush a sound rating for neglecting her children.

He found a young blackbird, whose parents had deserted it, a puffed-up ball of misery who was unable to find any food for itself. Dodder dug it worms from a mossy bank, taking care to kill the worm before giving it to the baby bird, just as he had seen the old birds do.

He fed this youngster for three days and gave it lessons how to fend for itself. He saved a whole family of field mice from a weasel, and when that little spring of steel, clothed in brown fur, swore and chittered at him, Dodder drew his knife and looked so terrifying that even the weasel had to retire. He found a baby bullfinch with a broken leg. He made a splint out of a pigeon's quill and mended it.

One result of these kind actions was that whenever he went hobbling along the river bank, he was followed by a string of baby things which clamoured to be fed. It would have done a Mortal good to see that funny little gnome with his peg leg and his kind wrinkled little face like a Pied Piper of Fairyland, followed by a procession of nondescript infants. They used to come and wait around Rumbling Mill for his appearance and as soon as he showed himself a shout would go up, 'Here comes Daddy Dodder,' and he would get no peace. The others laughed at him but Dodder was secretly delighted. There was nothing he liked more than helping the birds and beasts. Indeed, he was the most popular person in the district. His skill as a doctor spread like wildfire, and it was not very long before mothers brought their ailing children to him to ask him for advice. One mother thrush was very worried because her family was suffering from a common internal disorder. 'More greenfly, madam!' Dodder boomed at her. 'More greenfly! How can you expect them to be well? And try a spider, madam, if the trouble continues, there's nothing like a spider as a purge.' (Which is very true: a spider is as good as castor-oil.)

Taking advantage of this pause in their journey, Mrs Ben, despite all advice to the contrary, prevailed on her husband to consent to a family. She foolishly laid two eggs in the old Barnies' nest (with their permission, of course). But one night, when she had left them for an airing, a rat ate them, much to old Ben's secret relief. It was too late in the year, anyway, to start a family, and at any moment the ship would be ready and the gnomes would want to be moving on.

Occasionally Dodder would explore the cornfields, wandering about among the green forests which were so mysterious, and he would see the scarlet skirts of the poppies drooping over him, looking almost black against the evening sky.

Down among the cornstalks, Dodder chatted with harvest mice and field voles, enquired after their families and admired their cosy little nests. He passed the time of night with hedgehogs and frogs, and chatted with the moles about the dry hot weather. They had their runs deep down under the corn which led to the river. Moles are thirsty creatures and need to drink fairly frequently.

It was fascinating to stand or sit among those million, million cornstalks and hear the wind passing over, and to see the half-formed heads of grain, green as yet, bending and swaying all in unison.

Once his wandering took him to Bantley Heath where the Worm of Death lived (or used to live). The fact is, though not a soul knew about it, save a few startled lizards and mice, that two days after Cloudberry's disappearance, the Worm of Death set out again to keep a date with the young Barnies in Rumbling Mill. But a prowling fox had spied it and bitten it behind the head, and that was the end of the Worm of Death.

Dodder rambled through the furze and passed the very door of the adder's house. Even though it was now tenantless, evil was in the air and he was glad to be out of the wood.

Sometimes Squirrel accompanied him on these evening walks. Since his dreadful experience at Bantley Weir,

Squirrel was shy of water and he enjoyed accompanying Dodder on his 'rounds'.

They made a quaint pair, as they ambled along in those summer twilights, chatting together. Very often, after the day was over, the twain would get out the dinghy and row about among the lily beds, fishing for perch and roach, setting night lines, or simply lying up among the reeds. Dodder smoking and watching the gnats adancing, Squirrel pretending to catch imaginary fleas in his fluffy tail.

It sometimes happened that a boatload of Mortals passed by Rumbling Mill, but this was of rare occurrence, for even they seemed shy of Bantley Weir. And once they saw the river keeper walking among the buttercups, armed with a long pole with which he destroyed the moorhens' and dabchicks' nests. But needless to say, he never found the gnomes, and after he had gone Dodder and Squirrel would rescue the eggs—if they were unbroken by the staff—and replace them in the nest.

But the fishing season was at hand, for it was now the middle of June, and Otter said that there would soon be anglers about, especially near Bantley Weir. Moreover, Baldmoney pronounced that the *Jeanie Deans* was now fit for sea, and with every passing day the knowledge that they must be on the move once more became obvious.

This short holiday by the summer river was delightful, Rumbling Mill was a dangerously alluring Lotus Land. These halcyon days could not last for ever and Dodder felt in his bones that soon they must say goodbye to all at Rumbling Mill and continue their journey. Already there were signs that summer was well upon his golden-footed way.

The buttercups in the fields had begun to lose that first bright flush of varnished yellow and the starling families had left their nests and were down among the mowing grass, churring in their loud and insistent voices. The elder was in flower, another sign, and the crops were now coming into unripened ear.

Many early swallow families were out. They used to gather in a row on the mill-house roof, twittering ceaselessly, and that new music struck a strange uneasy chord within the memory. Dodder, when he heard them, remembered those autumn days on Poplar Island, when they were marooned there after the loss of the *Dragonfly*. And then the green summer trees and the lush water meadows seemed for an instant faded and brown, and he thought of the misty mornings and of the first gold spots in the elms along the hedgerows.

Somehow or another, the nightly gatherings and jolly suppers at Rumbling Mill now seemed to be more precious, more precious because everyone knew that time was getting short. The Otter cubs had developed into fine young creatures, swimming and diving almost as well as their parents, and the eldest had already caught his first fish unaided. One evening the Barnies summoned everyone to the loft to witness the young ones take their first real flight.

It was a great moment as the two anxious parents sat with them on the roof ridge and wheedled and coaxed the trembling owlets to trust themselves to the unstable air. The Otter cubs had been the same, their first plunge into water had been a nerve-racking experience.

The youngest owlet refused for a long time to launch away, not even the coaxing of Mrs Barny and the Bens could persuade it. And at last they had to call upon Dodder to use his influence. By kind words and reassuring motions, and a promise of a fat mouse all to itself from Mrs Barny, that terrified ball of woolly feathers launched itself, with a wild hoot, into the air.

It glided several hundred yards and landed upside down in an elder bush, panting but triumphant.

Baldmoney, who was as interested as any at this performance, seemed strangely moved. His eyes glistened when he saw the owlet gliding away and clapped his hands with delight. 'If only we could fly,' he said to Dodder, 'how *lovely* it would be! If only we had wings.'

But Dodder was not so sure. 'We aren't built for flying,' he grunted. 'I'd rather feel the firm earth supporting me, thank you!'

But afterwards Baldmoney was seen up in a corner, busy over his notebook, not speaking to anyone, and oblivious of the world.

As Squirrel remarked to Dodder, 'Old Baldy has some new Plan on the go. I was watching his face when the young owlets flew away. I believe he's got some mad hare-brained scheme he's working out, you mark my words!'

CHAPTER FIFTEEN

The Anchor Weighs

 do not know whether Dodder, in the quiet hours when he roamed alone through that dear country, ever entertained the idea of abandoning any further voyagings in the *Jeanie Deans*. It is unlikely. Once gnomes say they are going to do a thing, they do it. But I would hesitate to say that he was not tempted. Looking back on their Folly Brook days I think that Dodder may have realized that this lovely old ruined mill by the river, beset with trees and golden meadows, where the fish were weighty and the company was so congenial, was a good place to be. And now the River Folk had begun to accept them as one of themselves. Good friends form strong ties and Dodder knew this. He knew that the longer they stayed, the more these ties would bind them and the harder it would be to tear themselves away.

Never before had Dodder been able to do so much good and be such a help to all those pathetic little people who creep and run, walk and fly, whose existence depends so much on the whim of weather and twist of chance. By a kind act here, and a good deed there, Dodder had won the hearts of all at Rumbling Mill; it was a very, very happy place, upon which the sun always seemed to shine and where dark clouds were unknown.

But the Mortals, who had been noisy enough of latter years up the Folly Brook began even here in this remote spot to be noisily evident again. Strange lights hung in the sky at night, swinging balefully, like priests' censers. Curious rod-like beams sprang up and toyed with the stars, and sometimes red glares smouldered afar off, as of immense bonfires. Distant doors seemed to slam and the droning thunderbirds passed over, invisible but menacing.

One night, as they all sat under the wheelhouse after supper, laughing heartily at a new game invented by the young otters called 'Ben Knows Best', Rumbling Mill suddenly heaved up and groaned aloud from every ancient timber and joist. Tiles crashed loudly to the ground and the old rose-red chimney, after tottering and swaying for a split second like a drunken man, plunged down with an appalling splash into the mill pool, shearing away the peak of the gable and driving a shoal of perch quite frantic with terror.

This sudden shock was so terrifying, so outrageous, that for a moment or two everybody was frozen with fear. Then in a body they rushed from under the wheelhouse into the open air.

Dodder shook his head sadly. 'Dear, dear, dear, they *are* noisy tonight, bless their little hearts!' And Mrs Otter tried to comfort the young otters who were whimpering under a willow.

'It's all right, dears, it's only a thunderbird dropping its eggs.'

'We don't like thunderbirds,' sobbed one of the young otters. 'Why don't they lay their eggs somewhere else?'

Dodder sighed. 'I remember the time when there weren't such things as thunderbirds. Britain was much quieter then. I liked it better.'

'Let's go and see if the ship's all right,' suggested Baldmoney with a very anxious look on his face. So they all trooped along to her moorings. She was unharmed, though a flying slab of stone had narrowly missed her.

Rumbling Mill, shaken out of her four hundred odd years of peace and quietness, was full of dust and frightened cheeping mice. Dodder tried to calm them as well as he could and Ben, sitting on the mill top, called out that he would come down too and knock some sense into them, an offer which was not at all appreciated by the mice and which soon brought them to their senses. In an hour or two the incident was forgotten by most of them, but Dodder's mind had been definitely made up. Britain was no place now for the Little People and he thought of an island, far away in a grey lough, where no Mortal came and he sighed. A long, long way to travel, a weary way, o'er land and sea and mountain perhaps. But there was peace there, so Woodcock had told them, with no sound but the ripples on a stony shore and the cry of the Heaven Hounds upon their own restless journeyings. Woodcock was a very wise and sensible bird, Dodder had always had a great respect for him, a very silent bird, but with a tall head, full of wisdom.

A day or two later he thought the time had come to call a meeting—the last meeting, to discuss their plans and wind up their affairs and to say goodbye to all their many friends.

He sought out Baldmoney. The latter was tucked up in a dim corner muttering to himself and drawing busily. When he heard Dodder's approach he shut up his notebook and looked very self-conscious.

'Baldmoney.'

'Yes, Dodder?'

'I want a word with you in private. Tell Ben to come too, to the old punt in the Mill Leat.'

Baldmoney nodded and, putting his precious notebook in his pocket, he went to fetch Ben. That notebook he valued more than any other of his meagre possessions. He had, I am afraid, taken it off the workbench in Mr Shoebottom's workshop. The first three pages were filled with drawings and notes in Mr Shoebottom's handwriting, such as 'Two 350x17s, Bantley, Sat.' 'Five to One on Black Cap, nap, 2-15' and the mysterious remark, 'Spotted Cow, May 16, Bowling Club dinner' all of which was (naturally) Greek to Baldmoney.

When Ben had been found and summoned they trooped off to the punt among the weeds to hear what Dodder had to say. He stood up, cleared his throat and blew his nose.

'It's about Woodcock's island.'

Ben muttered 'Hum ha,' and nodded his head and looked very wise. Baldmoney said nothing.

'What happened the other night has sort of shaken me up,' continued Dodder. 'I think we've been inclined to let things slide lately. Well, that's not surprising. There's something about Rumbling Mill that makes one feel that way, and Otter and everyone have been so kind and jolly that it has been hard to think of other things. Well, what I've to say is this. We must start, start as soon as possible. You, Ben, know how far it is, 'cos Woodcock told you.'

'You mean to Woodcock's island?' asked Ben, blinking and scratching his beak bristles with one claw.

Dodder nodded. 'Yes, Woodcock's island. You all know as well as I do how the summer's getting on, and we must be getting on too. We've got to reach the sea and then we've got to get across to Woodcock's island, though *how* we're going to do that Pan only knows!'

Baldmoney seemed to be about to say something. He put his hand in his pocket for his notebook but after a glance at Dodder thought better of it and remained quite still.

'Well,' said Ben, after a pause, 'it's a good flip, a tidy flip.'

'You mean *step*,' corrected Dodder. 'We aren't birds, we haven't wings.'

'Step then,' said Ben. 'It's just the way you look at it.'

'What do you call a good step, Ben?'

Ben scratched his beak again, looked at Baldmoney out of the corner of his eye, winked, and then said, 'Oh, it'll take us into October if we start tomorrow.'

'October!' gasped Dodder. 'As long as that?'

''Fraid so,' said Ben gravely. 'That's if Baldmoney's plan works out all right.'

'And what *is* Baldmoney's plan?' asked Dodder rather impatiently.

'Don't ask that till we reach the sea,' said Ben, with an air of great finality. 'You'll only pooh-pooh the plan if we tell you now.'

Dodder grunted. 'Well, if you think we're going to sail across the Irish Sea in the *Jeanie Deans*, I'm staying right here at Rumbling Mill, cos it can't be done.'

'I don't suggest for a moment that we should!' burst out Baldmoney. 'I've a much better plan than that. I thought—' He caught Ben's eye and dried up. 'I thought . . . er . . . that is—'

'Thought what?' said Dodder. 'What are you stopping for?'

'Oh, nothing!'

'Very well then,' said Dodder a trifle huffily, 'you needn't tell me if you don't want to. I'll trust you both to see us safely there. If it had been one of Cloudberry's plans, now, I *should* have been uneasy.'

Baldmoney and Ben looked pleased at the compliment.

'Very well,' he continued, 'we'll start as soon as we can provision the ship. As you know, all the grain was spoilt at Bantley Weir. We've got to get fresh supplies aboard as soon as may be, and that's going to mean a lot of work. It's all right for you, Ben, you can pick up a mouse where you like and when you like, but we've got to rustle around. The acorns aren't ripe, which complicates matters. All we can do is to fish and fish for all we're worth, get 'em dried out and smoked, and then trust to luck. No doubt there'll be plenty to eat on Woodcock's island—I hope so anyway.'

The next few days were rather strenuous. There was all that bustle and activity one associates with impending departure. The young otters romped about, getting under people's feet, and then looking very solemn when they remembered they were not going too.

Many of the River Folk came to say goodbye and

thank Dodder for all he had done for them and one hedgehog completely broke down and went into hysterics. Otter had to pour water over her before she recovered. Otter fished and fished and the gnomes did too until they had amassed ample stores. The minnows, small dace, and roach were slit and dried, then smoked over a fire in the old mill house.

Squirrel ranged far and wide among the adjoining woodlands and came back with sackfuls of edible fungi and other delicacies dear to a squirrel's taste. Dodder's stock of wine, sadly depleted, was broken into for the final farewell supper on the last night at Rumbling Mill.

A great number of River Folk attended that farewell dinner and of course all the otters who had helped them raise the *Jeanie Deans* were asked and they attended, bringing with them relations of *theirs*, whom Otter or Mrs Otter had never met. But as there was enough for everyone it didn't matter, though, as Mrs Otter told her husband afterwards, it might have been very awkward.

Every water vole for miles around was invited, and the kingfishers, moorhens and grebes, and many reed and sedge warblers were asked too. Of course the owls had to be on their best behaviour and pretend that they never as much as *looked* at voles and mice, which was very comical because they pulled such funny innocent faces.

No less than fifteen hedgehogs arrived just before the meal (I had that from PeeWee the willow wren, so I believe it) and every Animal Banquet ever held paled before that sumptuous repast.

Bub'ms attended, though they hadn't been asked (bub'ms were considered rather 'rumty too' if you know what that means) and they all sat down (or perched) about the old threshing floor, there naturally being no room in the holt under the wheelhouse.

From first to last the whole thing went with a swing, and as many as liked sampled Dodder's excellent berry wines. When at last the feast was over, of course Dodder had to make one of his rather tedious speeches and everyone pretended to listen very reverently. One of the hedgehogs, who had had perhaps just too much of the wine, began to weep maudlin tears.

When the speech-making was over (Ben had to get up on a crossbeam and have his little say), Otter gave the toast of a good journey and a safe arrival. He made such a pretty speech there was even a tear in the bub'ms' eyes and then they all adjourned to the banks of the mill pool for a concert by the nightingales. This was a very good idea of Otter's, who had thought it all out beforehand. Some of the birds were suffering just a little from overeating but there were so many singing at once it didn't matter in the least, and the lovely notes floating out of the dark willows by the river bank were ravishing.

At last the party broke up; everybody voting it the best Animal Banquet that had ever been held. Yet, through it all, Dodder had to keep a very firm hand on his feelings, as you might well imagine.

And when the last bird had flown away and the last vole had waved goodbye they all went back to Rumbling Mill and helped Mrs Otter clean up the mess.

After the riotous time they had had, the place seemed suddenly forsaken and forlorn. Conversation was forced, subdued snuffles were heard from the young Otters and Barnies.

Dodder, buckling on his belt, found himself alone with old Otter and the two completely broke down, weeping, in each other's arms.

'C-c-come back, dear Dodder,' gulped Otter, when at last he could speak. 'You know that Rumbling Mill is always w-w-waiting f-f-for you and yours, if ever you return.'

With an effort Dodder mastered his feelings too. 'Goodbye, old friend, I'll think of you a lot and may Pan watch over you and keep you safely too!' Then he turned abruptly and hobbled out of the wheelhouse with a lump as big as an oak-apple in his throat.

It was 'all aboard' then. The last farewells were taken, Mrs Barny and Mrs Ben kissed each other by locking their bills in the owls' kiss, and the sight of this brought a smile to the lips of Dodder, who remembered the sight of the fighting owls falling into the nettles on their first night. He needed a sense of humour anyway, just then.

It was 'Anchor up!' and 'Let loose forrard,' and then came the clicking of the key.

'Goodbye, Otters, goodbye, Barnies! Pan keep you!'

'Pan keep you!' came back the answer from the fragrant river's gloom. And then the screws began to churn and inch by inch the gap between the side of the *Jeanie Deans* and the wheelhouse widened. The young Otters had made streamers out of Traveller's Joy, which they held in their teeth and one by one these became taut and broke as the ship drew farther from the bank, and as the bows turned ever outwards the Bens took off from the mill roof and floated away soaring with many a mournful hoot. Soon Rumbling Mill began to grow smaller in the moonlight until at last, with a final sigh, which was almost a groan from everyone, the dear old place was hidden by the willows.

The *Jeanie Deans* dropped down the silent river, once more bound upon her journey, a journey that had begun so long before at a place called Poplar Island, far away up the Folly Brook.

CHAPTER SIXTEEN

Exit Jeanie Deans

or a week after the sad farewell scene at Rumbling Mill, the *Jeanie Deans* made good progress. Of course the gnomes had plenty of excitement such as boatloads of Mortals, fishermen and such-like trifles. Once the wash of a steam launch nearly swamped them as they were hiding among the reeds. But their luck still held. At the rate they were going Dodder reckoned they would soon be nearing the sea. Ben and Baldmoney spent many hours poring over complicated plans. Dodder would often see them during the day (when, incidentally, Ben should have been sleeping) with the notebook laid on the cabin skylight and Baldmoney busy with his pencil. He sucked it a lot and stroked his beard and Ben would nod or shake his head at some remark of Baldmoney's and at times terrific arguments broke out. It was all very mysterious. Sometimes Dodder would pretend to see if there was anything on the fishing line which they always put out over the side when the ship was at anchor. He would stroll down the deck whistling and take sly sidelong glances at the busy pair, but when Baldmoney heard the familiar hobbling step he would shut up his notebook with a snap and remark in a loud voice to Ben 'that it seemed difficult to have any privacy these days'. Once Dodder managed to take a peep at the notebook when Baldmoney was away fishing but he could make nothing of it. Then something occurred which gave him an inkling what was in the wind. I have mentioned the thunderbirds which were really at the bottom of all their troubles. Every day they saw scores of them passing over, sometimes flying like Heaven Hounds in close formation, sometimes singly.

And whenever the familiar drone of their engines broke the silence Dodder would notice that Baldmoney seemed unusually interested. Of course, being very cunning, he pretended to take no notice of this new habit, but he began to have a vague suspicion that Baldmoney had some fantastic notion in his head of building a *flying machine*.

Now Dodder knew that such a thing was quite beyond the ingenuity of any gnome. Besides, what was the use? It would be better to persuade Sir Herne to take them over the sea, or even Ben. Had not Cloudberry once flown all the way to Spitzbergen on the back of a Heaven Hound? So why, in Pan's name, a *flying machine*? The more he thought about it the crosser he became. What was Baldmoney thinking of to entertain such an absurd idea? How could they ever make an engine? Really, it was quite beyond all common sense.

Supposing Baldmoney persisted in his crazy notion.

Supposing, when they reached the sea, he began to waste their precious time in building a thunderbird, what would happen? They would be stranded perhaps, right out on some desolate marsh with no woods and no cover and the winter would be upon them. They could never retrace their steps back to Rumbling Mill which, after all, did offer safe sanctuary and jolly company.

Poor old Dodder began to sleep badly; he began to wish they had never left Rumbling Mill at all. Each night when they weighed anchor he began to feel a cold fear clutch at his heart. Every beat of the screws was taking them away from security into the dread unknown and a freezing death on some lonely strand.

It soon became apparent that he must say something to Baldmoney and he made up his mind that if his fears proved correct he would absolutely refuse to go another yard. Even if they had to walk all the way back to Rumbling Mill, he would refuse to go any farther down the river to certain death by exposure.

If only Ben had made some arrangements with the birds then he would not have worried so much. He knew how easy it was to ride on Sir Herne's back, for instance. He remembered how once on his journey up the Folly to join the others, in those early days of exploration, how Sir Herne had given him a ride. Of course it was terrifying enough, but he had enjoyed it—afterwards. To trust the whole party to one of Baldmoney's crazy inventions was asking too much. He would not entertain the idea for a moment.

So one hot afternoon when he spied the conspirators busy as usual over the notebook, Dodder plucked up his courage and decided to have it out with them.

He knocked out his pipe and came stumping down the deck, trying to appear at his ease.

'Can't get any peace nowadays,' said Baldmoney with a sniff as he heard Dodder's footsteps on the decking.

Ben gave a wink and scratched behind his ear in an irritable fashion and the twain waited patiently for Dodder to pass by.

'I want a word with you both,' said Dodder, 'now I've got you here together. Of course I know what you're going to say, that it's none of my business, and that my job is to steer the ship and take you safely to the sea. Well, we can't be far off now and I think you ought to tell me what plans you've got.'

A silence ensued. Ben made a sort of muffled hoot in his throat and looked at Baldmoney. Baldmoney looked at Ben and seemed acutely uncomfortable.

'We'll tell you when we get there,' said Baldmoney at last. 'There's no need for you to worry us like this.'

Dodder's face grew red with anger, and Ben looked as though he wished himself miles away in some quiet ivy-clad oak.

'I must insist on knowing,' said Dodder. 'I'm the leader of this expedition and if you won't tell me then we'll go no farther—not a single mile will we go, so there!'

Baldmoney heaved a deep sigh and looked glumly at Ben for guidance. Ben shook his head and looked the other way. Dead silence ensued.

A fish splashed out in the river and a mother moorhen swam past with a whole string of sooty wheezing chicks valiantly struggling after.

'You talk to him, Ben,' whispered Baldmoney.

'Well,' said Ben clearing his throat nervously, 'we can't tell you yet, we really can't, because our plans aren't quite cut and dried.'

'And if you won't go on,' broke in Baldmoney, 'then you'll have to stay behind. Sneezewort, Squirrel, and the Bens will go with me to Woodcock's island and—and—well, that's all we've got to say. I'm sorry, but there it is.'

Dodder stumped off without a word and as soon as he was out of earshot Baldmoney heaved another sigh. 'I *knew* it! I knew it! Dodder's going all crusty now because we won't tell him. If we do he'll be just the same, I know him so well. If we tell him what our plan is he'll still say he won't go another yard. It was just the same when we made our boat, the *Dragonfly*, you remember; he said it was all poppycock and that he'd stay at home. He's as stubborn as anything.'

Ben apprehensively eyed the distant figure of Dodder who was elaborately pulling up one of the fishing lines over the stern. 'D'you *really* think he means what he says—d'you *really* think he'll refuse to weigh anchor tonight? If so, we're in the soup. It's a long way still to the sea and it's farther to Rumbling Mill and that's what the old fellow is thinking of. Anyway, the *Jeanie Deans* can't go back upriver against this current. We're in a fine old mess, if you ask me.'

'D'you think Squirrel could knock some sense into him?' asked Baldmoney. 'We can't leave the old thing behind, even though we said we would; it wouldn't be half the fun without him and I believe he knows it. Oh dear, what *are* we to do?' Baldmoney drummed his fingers on the skylight.

Meanwhile, as Dodder pulled up the fishing line, he found his head was in a whirl. So they wouldn't tell him even now, when he said he would go no farther. He had thought at least that Ben would have told him. Was he being unreasonable? he asked himself. He remembered the time he had been left behind at the Oak Tree and how miserable he was. Now he had said he would go no farther he must stick to his word. It was all very awkward. At last an idea struck him. Why not ask Baldmoney point-blank if they intended to build a thunderbird? If Baldmoney answered in the negative they could go on; if he said they *were* going to build one then he was justified in refusing to go any farther. Yes, the more he thought of the idea, the more he liked it.

He pulled up the wet line, re-baited, and flung it out once more. Then he turned round and went stumping down the deck to Ben and Baldmoney who were still sitting on the skylight looking the picture of misery.

'I've been thinking over what I said,' said Dodder to them, 'and there's one more thing I'm going to ask you: I've a notion what your plan is and I'm going to ask you straight out! Is it a flying machine you have in mind? If it is then what I said earlier holds good. The ship goes no farther tonight. If it isn't, then we'll weigh anchor at sundown, same as usual. Will you answer me that? Is it a thunderbird you're going to build?'

Dodder noticed a look of relief pass over Baldmoney's face. 'I'll answer you that, Dodder, it isn't a thunderbird, is it, Ben?'

Ben, who still seemed rather uncomfortable, shook his head. 'No, it isn't a thunderbird, Dodder, cross my mouse-tails it isn't!'

It was Dodder's turn to look relieved. 'Right, then I'll believe you, and I'm glad, because I know you could never build one, not if you tried for ever so long.'

'Of course we couldn't build a thunderbird!' exclaimed Baldmoney. 'How could we? What made you think we could?'

'I've seen you looking at them a lot,' confessed Dodder, grinning for the first time for days. 'Every time one goes over I see you take a good look and then rush off to your notebook, that's why I thought you meant to build one. You're clever, Baldmoney, but not clever enough for that, I know a gnome's capabilities! Well,' he went on, 'now we've cleared the air a bit we'll see how Sneezewort's getting on with the supper because we'll weigh anchor at last light.' And away went the funny little man whistling the tune of the 'Gnomes' Shanty'.

Baldmoney looked at Ben, Ben looked at Baldmoney.

'We told him the truth, didn't we?' said the former. 'It isn't a thunderbird, is it?'

'No, I suppose not,' said Ben, 'not a *real* thunderbird.' He was a very truthful owl and he still seemed a little uncomfortable.

'Well, now off you go and have a good sleep, Ben,' said Baldmoney. 'You look tired out, old bird, and this strong light is bad for your eyes. Mrs Ben will be wondering where you are, I'll be bound.'

As soon as supper was over and all the things had been washed up (Mrs Ben came along and gave them a claw), the anchor was weighed and the *Jeanie Deans* set out.

The bats were already abroad and all the fishermen had gone home leaving little crumpled scraps of cast paper and crusts of bread on the bank, round which the water voles were gathering. It was too late also for boats to be out, even the loving couples had gone home, and the gnomes had the river to themselves. It was a perfect night, windless and full of stars.

The Bens, as usual, had gone off downriver ahead of the ship, picking up a mouse here and there around the stackyards. As for the gnomes and Squirrel, they had dined well.

White mists lay like fine-drawn veils about the water meadows and many mallards were busy, quacking and flying above reedy backwaters.

Cows stared at them as they went by. Nearly all were lying down, their big mouths moving sideways as they chewed the cud, and numberless cockchafers boomed to and fro, sometimes banging into the boat. One big fellow hit the funnel an awful crack and lay insensible for quite a time on the bridge, much to Dodder's annoyance.

Dodder was now much more happy in his mind. He knew Baldmoney and Ben would not tell him a lie, so it was not a thunderbird after all; so what *could* it be? Still, he wouldn't raise the matter again, and he had not forgotten that Pan was watching over them; *he* would see they came to no harm surely.

He puffed contentedly at his pipe and watched the dark cliff of a willow swim towards them and pass slowly astern. Somehow there was a strong hint of late summer in the air. In the flat river meadows the hay had been cut and carted, the aftermath was already springing green. And the buttercups had gone and the elder with them, no longer did their sweet smell make the night air heavy. In the luminous darkness the meadowsweet lining the river bank seemed very white and glow-worms gleamed in the damp grass. At the end of the summer, you may have noticed that there is a peculiar smell about the fields; it isn't that first fresh smell, and mingled with it is the faint tang of cattle and sheep and mature plants and leaves.

And the swallows too, they were beginning to band together. It wouldn't be long before the harvest. Dodder sighed. There would be no more moonlight expeditions to glean the wheaten ears from Lucking's fields below Moss Mill: it was all very sad.

Far ahead he heard the Bens hooting and in a few moments he saw the black silent shapes appear on their starboard beam.

Both birds came to rest, Mrs Ben on the ship's mast and Ben upon the bridge. They came quite noiselessly and alighted so gently that the *Jeanie Deans* only gave a faint rock and never altered course.

'Bad news,' said Ben briefly. 'Shut off your engines, Dodder.'

Dodder pushed the lever and the beat of the screw stopped abruptly. Only the chuckle of water along the sides of the ship broke the silence.

'There's a big weir ahead,' said Ben. 'Bigger than any we've come across yet and to go over will be asking for trouble—in fact, it would be suicide!'

'Make fast,' grunted Dodder to Baldmoney, who ran to the bow of the ship. Squirrel jumped ashore and tied the *Jeanie Deans* up to a reed stem.

'Let's go and have a look at it,' said Dodder, making for the gangway which, in the meantime, had been lowered by the obliging Sneezewort. They all trooped ashore and crept down the bank. The grass was high and wet with dew, masses of willow herb made the going hard. Soon they heard the dull thunder of the great weir, which grew louder as they approached.

It was a beautiful sight in the moonlight: the eerie tossing manes of white foam, the ghastly eddies and foam clots, the slowly revolving rafts of broken reed, endlessly swinging in circles in the backwaters.

Across the river, almost opposite the weir, was a cottage and behind it a clump of magnificent poplars. But the sound of the night wind, which had sprung up in the last hour and was playing in those silvered columns, was drowned by the tumult of the falling waters. The gnomes had to shout to make themselves heard.

'We'll never make it,' bawled Dodder in Baldmoney's ear.

Baldmoney nodded his head and his face was very miserable. Ben, who had meanwhile been sitting on one of the big wooden posts of the weir itself, wagged his big head at them, as though it was no good thinking of ever risking the descent in such a Niagara of waters.

After standing a while looking at the rushing river as though they thought some miracle would happen, they turned back and made their way towards the anchored boat, the sound of the weir dying behind them.

Dodder wagged his head. 'Ben's right, we're in a fix. I don't know what to do. If only the otters were here we might have portaged round it but we can't do it by ourselves, even with Squirrel's help.'

'I don't see why we shouldn't try,' said the latter animal, who all the time had been skipping about in the moonlight, 'we got her out of Shoebottom's shop.'

'That was different,' replied Dodder. 'There was a hard

road and the ground sloped. It's tough going here with all this willow herb and boggy ground. There's only one thing I can think of and that is to cut the boat adrift and let her take her chance and try and salvage her below the weir. There *is* a chance she will not sink, especially if we batten her down.'

This really seemed the only solution and after much arguing they decided to take this course. Baldmoney and Sneezewort volunteered to go out in the dinghy below the weir and try to take the *Jeanie Deans* in tow. The portaging of the dinghy was an easy matter for them and without delay this was done. They untied it from the stern and carried the little boat well below the weir. They found the effort all they could manage through the thick herbage. After seeing Baldmoney and Sneezewort push out into the calm water, Dodder went back to the anchored ship. His heart was very heavy as he untied the rope. If the *Jeanie Deans* was to be wrecked a second time the outlook was pretty black and their chances of continuing their journey very remote.

For some time the little gnome sat among the rushes with the rope in his hands. He could feel the pull of the river like some subtle monster trying to draw the *Jeanie Deans* away. It was really an awful moment. It was like saying goodbye to a very dear and well-loved friend and they had come to regard the ship as part of themselves. In it they had shared so many joys and sorrows and braved so many dangers and adventures. Then, with a prayer to Pan, Dodder let go the rope and sat there, drawn by an awful fascination as the ship slowly, slowly receded from the reeds. There she was now, going out into mid-river, drifting helplessly round and round. Sometimes he saw her full length, the empty bridge with no figure at the wheel, the vacant decks, the funnel shining in the moonlight. They had taken from her hold some of the things they treasured most—their spare moleskin coats, their fishing rods and gear, the Acorn Hop board and many another cherished possession, but their pictures they had to leave.

Now she was bow on, appearing half her size, and all the time she was sliding down towards that dreadful weir. Dodder found that he had to run to keep up with her, a difficult matter with his bone leg. Soon he was panting and puffing, for it was a hot night, and he fought the willow herb stems which seemed to purposefully bar his way. Soon the vegetation hid her from view and he saw the dear ship no longer.

Meanwhile, Baldmoney and Sneezewort, waiting in the dinghy below the weir, gazed with straining eyes upstream. Ben was visible now and again, wheeling on slow wings against the stars, obviously keeping watch on the helpless drifting ship.

Their eyes were glued on the white crest of the distant weir whose dull thunder reached them. And then they saw a tiny black object appear at the top. In a second it vanished from view amidst the foam and tossing spray and the awful minutes ticked by and no boat reappeared. Ben circled and circled again, hooting mournfully, and soon Sneezewort began to snivel.

'She's gone down,' he sobbed. 'We shall never, never see her again. Oh! why did we ever do it? Why? Oh! why?'

Baldmoney did not reply. 'Row nearer,' he said, but

their puny efforts were of no avail against the quickened current of the river and they fell back again and again.

Ben came gliding over. 'It's no good, gnomes, she's gone to the bottom,' he called down to them. 'I *knew* she would! I told you so!' And alas what Ben said was true.

The *Jeanie Deans* had at last come to the end of her adventures, her last voyage had been made.

A sunken bar of iron at the foot of the fall (round which was tangled many a fisherman's trace and line) had pierced the bowels of their faithful ship, and there, transfixed below the seething bubbles at the weir foot, she was gradually being pounded into little pieces. First her funnel went, then the bridge and all her superstructure. Her plates were riven apart, the bunks and woodwork split and shattered.

Soon, as Baldmoney and Sneezewort sorrowfully rowed towards the shore, they beheld an exhausted and weeping Dodder staggering along the bank.

And all the comforting words of the Bens and Squirrel and his brother gnomes, could not take those tears away. The little man seemed utterly broken; he sat rocking to and fro among the dewy grass, his whole minute frame shaken by sobs.

It was all very sad and unfortunate but, as Ben pointed out, if they had all been aboard her they might have been drowned and that would have indeed been a terrible thing. Though the future seemed black they had at least their lives and perhaps something would turn up, as it had done in the past, to give them renewed hope and courage to carry them to their journey's end.

CHAPTER SEVENTEEN

Baldmoney Gets to Work

rom what Peewee the willow wren told me, the loss of the *Jeanie Deans* was a severe blow to everyone concerned. The news of the accident filtered through to the Stream People back at Rumbling Mill. But of course that was a long time afterwards and it was too late for the otters to do anything about it, otherwise I am sure they would have set out at once to render assistance to their friends, even though they were so far away. It's surprising, though, how news gets about; bird tells bird, water vole tells vole, some chance remark by a King of Fishers perhaps, and soon *everybody* knows! You may be sure the good ship was mourned, as well she might be, but everyone who heard the news did the same thing, they heaved a sigh of relief and said, 'Well, there's one thing, souls, the gnomes are safe.' And that was the general opinion, which just goes to show how high Dodder and his brothers stood (and do not let us forget Squirrel and the Bens) in the estimation of the Stream People. Of course the real truth of the Cloudberry incident never leaked out. The Worm of Death, being dead himself, was the only one who had known the truth, which we may say was a very good thing. Cloudberry had never been so popular as his fellows but it would have cast a slur on the good name of gnomes in general had the facts become known.

Now it would have made a lot of difference had there been kind friends to comfort the little men when they lost their fine ship. It is true, they had the Bens and Squirrel, but the wild people take a little knowing, you have to live with them, as the gnomes had done at Oak Tree Pool or Rumbling Mill, before there is intimacy or friendship.

The scene of the dreadful disaster described in the last chapter was called Windover Weir. I mention the fact because it plays an important part in this story in so far as it is the place where Baldmoney became a hero and the saviour of them all. It was a pretty place, though not wild and forsaken like Rumbling Mill, and everything was on a much grander scale. On either side were rich water meadows with a dear little village and church with a steeple spire hidden in elms only a mile from the weir. It was a favourite resort for picnic parties (human ones, of course; no animals would ever hold a meeting there for that reason). There was the little cottage hard by where the man lived who looked after the weir and controlled the water and his name was Nathaniel Threadgold. He had a wife, a portly rosy-faced woman with a moustache, and their cottage was called Windover Cottage. Nathaniel suffered from rheumatics, as he was always getting wet, but they were a very happy couple. They kept hens (white ones), a pig, and two black-and-white goats which were always tethered in the little apple orchard behind the cottage. And the goats had two little kids, dear creatures, who were always up to some tricks or other. In the winter Mr Threadgold kept them in a byre, or shed, at the end of the meadow, but in summer he left them out all night. It was not very long before the goats and kids became firm friends of the gnomes and very useful they proved to be; for, in addition to helpful advice, the nanny-goat supplied the little men with plenty of milk and asked for nothing in return.

When the *Jeanie Deans* did not reappear from the uneasy depths of Windover Weir, the Bens and Squirrel had a hard time trying to comfort the three gnomes. The latter were so prostrated with grief they swore that they would go no farther, that after a rest of a day or two in some quiet spot they would retrace their steps, and take up their abode with their old friends at Rumbling Mill.

Of course this was really impossible because they could never have trudged back all those miles before summer's end and Ben pointed this out to them. 'No,' said the wise good bird, 'don't do that; take my advice and find some snug spot hard by the river here and settle down for the winter. We'll look after you, we'll see you come to no harm, and then in the spring you can make your way back to Rumbling Mill!'

And so after many more tears and arguments (some of them very heated) they cast about for some temporary home. As usual, Ben came to the rescue. He knew a little quiet lane, he said, not half a mile from the river, which was the very thing. It had steep banks crowned with old thick hawthorns and sloe bushes and nobody ever passed that way save when, in the autumn, the sloes were ripe. Then Mrs Threadgold would go there with the goats to gather them (the goats followed the Threadgolds about like dogs). Her sloe gin was famous, as many an Oxford undergraduate could testify.

Ben had learnt all this from the nanny-goat, to whom he had told the whole story.

And so it was that at last Dodder was won over and everyone trooped over the night meadows to see the place.

It certainly was a very secluded and exclusive spot; Dodder took to it at once. The hawthorn roots were coiled like snakes and stuck out in ledges and cables from the steep banks and under them were caverns and caves as snug as anything. Moreover, ground ivy was very plentiful, and ferns, cowslips, hemlock, lady's smocks and brambles completely screened these secret places and hollows from any prying gaze.

As for Baldmoney and Sneezewort (and Squirrel too) they fell in love with the place. 'As snug a hedge as ever I did see!' exclaimed Baldmoney, and Ben who was sitting by on a fence post nodded his head like a mandarin's as much as to say, 'What did I tell you!'

True, it was a bit of a come-down to live in a hedge

172

after Rumbling Mill or the Oak Tree House. In the old, old days the gnomes who dwelt in hollow trees regarded themselves as a cut above Hedge Gnomes, but as there were no Hedge Gnomes left it didn't matter very much.

And better still, very soon after they arrived, a dormouse called and made their acquaintance. She was a dear little soul, as round as a golf ball and so friendly. And it was she who introduced them to a hedge-pig and it was the hedge-pig who whispered in an awed voice to Dodder that just up the lane a little way there lived a fern-bear or badger.

'Well, let's go and see him,' said Dodder at once, 'and present our compliments. I've a notion that if we've got to stay here for the winter he'll give us some help.'

So, with the dormouse and the hedge-pig leading, the whole party called on Mr Brockett. They caught him just emerging from his front door under a screen of ferns and after Hedgepig had explained their visit and how the gnomes had lost their boat, he seemed overjoyed. As a matter of fact, Mr Brockett led a very lonely life up Sperrywell Lane, as lonely as Squirrel's had been in Crow Wood. After all, dormice and hedgehogs and the like are very good and worthy people, but you cannot carry on an intelligent, sustained conversation with them. Gnomes and squirrels were an entirely different cup of tea.

'Come in, come in,' he said, when Hedgepig had faltered through his story. 'I'm a lonely old bachelor and I've lived here all by myself for more years than I care to remember. Only too delighted to help you all I can. Come in, come in, all of you!'

They followed him down into his underground fortress and as they stumbled along in the gloom, Baldmoney nudged Dodder and whispered, 'Not so bad, what?' and Dodder whispered back, 'We're in luck, I do believe!'

'Have some honey,' said Mr Brockett, sitting down like a large woolly bear on a bed of bracken. 'I've some lovely honey!'

The gnomes made polite sounds and Sneezewort, who had forgotten to remove his hat, was given a terrific dig in the ribs by Squirrel.

'I heard all about your journey up the Folly,' said Mr Brockett, when everyone had set to with a will and sounds of suckings and smackings filled the gloom.

'You heard all about it?' exclaimed Dodder, looking very surprised, licking first one finger then the other. 'Whoever told you?'

'Oh, I forget. I get about a lot at night you know, mucking around Windover Weir. Someone told me, a vole or somebody, or perhaps it was Dabchick. Yes, now I come to think of it, it was Dabchick told me. But I thought there were four of you. Where's the other one?'

'Oh, you mean Cloudberry,' said Dodder. 'Well . . . Cloudberry began to be very difficult, very difficult indeed and . . . well . . . er . . . he went off again one night and we haven't seen him since. He always was such a fellow for going his own way, didn't seem able to settle down anywhere.'

'Well,' said Badger, 'since you have honoured me with a visit I can only say that Pan must have brought you here to cheer up a poor lonely old creature! I shall be more than delighted to welcome you here to Sperrywell Lane and you can live in my house as long as you wish. It will be warm in the winter and then perhaps if you want to go back to Rumbling Mill you can, but for my part, I'd much rather you stayed here with me. Everything I have is yours and any advice I can give you is more than welcome. I suppose I know this part of the country better than most.'

The gnomes made polite noises in their beards, Sneezewort grinned, and Ben nodded his head and winked at Squirrel.

All this shows how kind the animals were to one another. In the same way Squirrel had welcomed the gnomes to share his drey in Crow Wood and now, to think of the gnomes living apart from the Bens was quite unthinkable. All this made for a certain cosiness. Shelter from the weather, warmth, and plenty of nice things to eat, these things drew the refugees together.

As Mr Brockett had so graciously given them the run of his house, the gnomes were delighted. Yet if it was to be their winter quarters it lacked one essential thing for complete 'snugness', and that was a fire. Mr Brockett had seen fires made by Humans, he had seen bonfires in the fields in the autumn time and had even warmed himself by their dying embers in the quiet of autumn nights, but he had never contemplated having one to sit by in his own home. So that when the enterprising Baldmoney suggested that they should make a chimney to carry off the smoke, Mr Brockett was very dubious. Yet the gnomes painted such wonderful pictures of their Animal Banquets at Oak Tree House and of the good times they had there that the old gentleman began to be quite excited at the prospect, because fern-bears like nothing better than to be cosy in the winter months; they are the cosiest animals on four legs and very clean too in their habits.

So they set to work, Badger burrowing with his big claws, and the gnomes taking their turn with pointed pieces of wood. It took a long time to drill that hole and they had to call in the help of a couple of local moles to finish the job. The shaft of the chimney came out inside a decayed ash stump growing in the bank above. When it was finished the gnomes lit a fire and it was quite an excitement for them, and especially for Badger, who was beside himself with delight, vowing that he would never go to sleep in the cold weather, as he had always done so hitherto. He sat and warmed his furry stomach and dozed in the genial warmth just as though it was bitter January time. The flue drew beautifully and they followed the principle they had adopted in the Oak Tree House of never lighting their fire save on windy wild nights when the smell of the smoke or the sight of it would not be noticed.

And in addition to this great luxury, Baldmoney and the others got busy making shelves in the subterranean galleries and fitting an inner door of oak wood to keep out the night air.

All this might have appeared unnecessary to the casual passer-by as it was still summer time and it was hard to imagine that winter ever came to that dreamy and secluded spot. Yet the blackberries were reddening on the brambles, which showed that winter was not so very far away.

Not only that; Dodder, returning from one of his nightly fishing expeditions at Windover Weir, came burdened with a hatful of gorgeous mushrooms. These were duly fried and eaten for supper the next night, but Badger, after tasting one, spat it out and vowed he would never taste another.

Squirrel was the one for mushrooms and he knew other edible fungi which were just as nice or nicer. It is not generally known that squirrels eat many wild fungi in the woods and are passionately fond of them.

Of course Dodder brought in some fine catches of fish which were smoked over the fire; in fact, it was quite like old times in Oak Tree House.

Mr Brockett never tired of hearing of the great adventure up the Folly and of all the happenings in Crow Wood. To tell the truth, the old fellow sometimes reflected to himself as he went about his nightly hunting, how pleasant his life had become and how he enjoyed the company of his new-found guests. He even blessed the night the *Jeanie Deans* foundered at Windover Weir, for if the accident had not happened he would never have seen the gnomes and would have continued in his old way of life.

Occasionally he was accompanied on his nightly wanderings by Baldmoney and Sneezewort, and even Squirrel gave up his beauty sleep to go with him. As soon as the first stars began to show they would go trotting off, up the dusky tunnel of Sperrywell Lane and out into the open water meadows where the mists lay in thick white layers. Once they met a wood dog (which was their name for a fox) but as Mr Brockett was with them the sinister beast passed by with wrinkled lip and wicked sneer. Mr Brockett had never liked foxes, they were dirty, evil-smelling beasts, and since he had heard of the episode of Sneezewort and the wood dog up the Folly Brook, his opinion of them had been even lower.

Many a chat they had with the goats in the orchard, though Mr Brockett would not go near the cottage; it was a rule he had made and a very wise one too: 'Keep clear of Man dwellings'.

Every night either Dodder or Sneezewort would go and milk the nanny, bringing home the rich rather goaty-flavoured milk in cunning little wooden pails they had made. It was wonderful the way those gnomes transformed Mr Brockett's house into a comfortable residence. Every convenient corner held a cupboard, beautifully made, complete with a door which fastened. In them they stored all kinds of things: mushrooms and smoked minnows, various edible wild fruits, and all the precious odds and ends they had saved from the *Jeanie Deans*. I forgot to mention that Dodder had even salvaged some of the little wine shells, but when he tapped one of them he found that the water had got in, probably when the ship was sunk at Bantley Weir, and the wine was spoiled. But as the elderberries were just coming on, Dodder used to spend many hours of the day preparing the berries so he was kept pretty busy. Sneezewort helped him and also did most of the cooking and collecting of firewood, so these two were well employed.

Once Baldmoney had finished making numerous shelves and cupboards he found himself without very much to occupy his days. He frequently went fishing, but to tell you the truth, much of his time was spent in Ben's company. Ben and he would sit for hours with their heads together, sometimes sitting on the top bar of a gate or stile or an old tree stump. It was obvious that the mysterious plan was still being discussed and that Baldmoney, at any rate, had no intention of spending the winter at Sperrywell Lane.

About thirty yards from Mr Brockett's front door, deep among the bracken, Ben and Baldmoney had found a sandy cavity where the roots of the sloe bushes overhung, forming a natural ceiling. Baldmoney called it his workshop, but he said no word about it to either Sneezewort or Squirrel and he was very careful to say nothing to Dodder about it. The only other person who was let into the secret was Yaffle, a green woodpecker, who lived in a tall ash tree at the top of the lane. Yaffle was a very fine fellow with a military bearing. He had a beautiful suit of green feathers, a thick black moustache and a crimson top to his head. He was an expert on timber and from him Baldmoney had learnt all he knew of carpentry.

Under cover of darkness, or during the day when Dodder and Sneezewort were busy in Mr Brockett's house, the three conspirators would foregather in the workshop and muffled hammerings might be heard at times and sounds of drilling and boring.

Yaffle could be seen flying towards Sperrywell Lane with long pieces of wood in his bill and Baldmoney paid frequent visits to the tall reed beds by the riverside, returning laden with lengths of cut tough reed.

The truth cannot be hidden any longer from you, they were making a machine which outwardly closely resembled an aeroplane! And I must say that it was being made with the most exquisite skill. In length it was no less than three feet long and the span of its wings stretched from one side of the workshop to the other. The framework of the body was being built in sections and firmly morticed together, and inside the body were little bucket seats made from hollow reeds and one big seat halfway down which was four times the size of the others.

Squirrel had been surprised one day when Baldmoney

asked him his waist measurement. Squirrel said that he hadn't the slightest idea and Baldmoney had measured him. Squirrel thought that Baldmoney was making him a suit of clothes and told him that it would be a waste of time, he had never worn clothes and didn't intend to begin now. Pan had given him an all-weather suit of fur and it would be a waste of time. Baldmoney chuckled and said he had had a bet with Ben about Squirrel's waist measurement and he wanted to make sure. But all the same, Squirrel was very suspicious and kept his eyes open.

Meanwhile, day by day and night by night the framework of Baldmoney's invention was pieced together, until the whole machine was completed, bar the covering of the spars and struts.

It had two doors, one on either side of the body or fuselage and you may be sure that Baldmoney had let himself go on cupboards and such-like. Later he had to take some of these out again, because of the increased weight. Ben, who knew all about aeronautics, implored Baldmoney to cut down such luxuries to a minimum.

'It's no good, Baldy, you must keep her light or she'll never be airborne.'

And Baldmoney would sorrowfully undo the work of hours. After all, Ben knew best.

At last, towards the end of July, the skeleton of the machine was completed. And then came the problem of finding a waterproof covering of some sort, which was both light and tough. It really was a problem and many suggestions were made.

Yaffle suggested leaves, which was stupid, and Ben was inclined to think that mouses' skins might serve but it would have been a long business catching enough mice and stitching the pelts together. Besides, as Baldmoney pointed out, when the skins became wet the weight of the machine would be so great that it would never fly.

In despair Baldmoney thought of the goats, Mr Threadgold's goats. They were always ready to be helpful and after consulting with Ben and Yaffle, Baldmoney decided he would let them into the secret. So it was agreed and on the twenty-fifth night of July the three conspirators slipped away to Mr Threadgold's orchard.

CHAPTER EIGHTEEN

Wonderbird

hey found the goats asleep under the apple trees. There was little moon, but against the stars the unripened apples were clearly visible.

Baldmoney stole up to the sleeping nanny and poked her gently on the nose.

'Nanny-goat! Nanny-goat! Wake up please, we want your advice.'

'Hey! what's that you say? Who is it?'

'Baldmoney and Ben—we've come to ask your advice on a very important matter, and we're very sorry to disturb you at this late hour.'

'Not at all, not at all,' said the good-natured creature. 'Go ahead.'

'First of all,' said Baldmoney, 'we must ask you to keep what we are going to tell you a complete secret. We don't want a word breathed to anyone, least of all Dodder and Sneezewort.'

The nanny-goat nodded her head.

'Well, it's this. Ben and I here are making a Wonderbird, which we hope will be the means of us reaching Woodcock's island.'

'Yes,' said the nanny-goat, 'I understand, I know all about your journey, of course, because Ben told everything and how you lost your ship at Windover Weir.'

'Well, the fact of the matter is, that we've got her pretty well made, but we're stuck for one thing and that's some sort of light, waterproof fabric with which to cover the framework. We've thought of everything: leaves, skins and so forth, but all are unsuitable. It must be able to keep out the wet, you understand, and not be too heavy.'

'Um,' said the goat, getting slowly to her feet, 'let me think now. It's no good asking my husband, *he* never has any ideas. Well,' said she, after a long pause, 'it seems to me you want some sort of light material. Now what about one of Mr Threadgold's shirts?'

'Mr Threadgold's shirts!' exclaimed Baldmoney. 'But what would Mr Threadgold say? We can't take the shirt off his back, can we? I agree that some such material is what we want; it would be light and tough, but would it be waterproof?'

'Ah! that's the question,' said the goat, 'that I don't know. He wears his shirts in all weathers, so I suppose it must be.'

'Yes, but we've got to get hold of his shirt first,' said Ben. 'That won't be an easy matter, I'll wager.'

'As easy as eating fallen apples,' replied the goat. 'There's one of his shirts hanging on the line now behind the cottage. Why not go and see?'

'But it's stealing,' said Baldmoney. 'We gnomes never steal, not from anyone.'

'Well, anyway, why not go and have a look at it,' said the goat, 'and come back and let me know.'

So off Baldmoney went to the cottage and Ben, flying after, perched on top of the post which held the clothes-line.

Mrs Threadgold had forgotten to take in the washing and a whole line of it hung there against the stars.

With a cautious look at the blind uncurtained windows of the cottage, which seemed to be watching them from the bowers of red rambler roses, Baldmoney went up the post as nimbly as a harvest mouse. He wormed his way along the line, ignoring three pairs of socks, two pairs of stockings, a petticoat belonging to Mrs Threadgold, a pair of pants and drawers, until he came to Mr Threadgold's shirt. It was certainly a beautiful shirt, a blue linen one, and the more Baldmoney felt its texture and the more he looked at it, the more he felt sure it was the very thing.

'I don't like stealing,' said Baldmoney to Ben, who all this time had been watching from the top of the post, 'but I can't see that we shall ever find anything else, which will do as well.'

And then, giving way to temptation, he pulled the clothes pegs and the fine blue garment fluttered like a tired ghost to the grass below. Rolling it quickly up, and with a guilty glance back at the cottage, they hurried back to the orchard and spread the shirt out upon the ground.

'It's certainly a lovely shirt,' sighed Baldmoney.

'The very thing,' said Ben. 'We shall have to have it, there's no other way.'

'Have it then,' said the goat, as though the shirt were her property. 'He has plenty more and I'm sure he wouldn't mind you using it if he knew the facts.'

'I don't like taking it—it's a Pixie Trick, but there's no other way out . . .' Baldmoney slowly rolled up the shirt and hoisted it on to his back.

Next morning when Mrs Threadgold went out to bring in the washing she gasped in astonishment. Mr Threadgold's best Sunday shirt had completely vanished, only the two clothes-pegs lay on the grass below. 'Well I never did!' she exclaimed. 'Where can it be?'

She searched all over the orchard and all about the cottage. Then she ran in to tell her husband who was just finishing his breakfast of ham and eggs.

'Have you tuk your best shirt off the line, Nathaniel?'

'Me best shirt? No, not I!'

'Then it's bin stole!' gasped Mrs Threadgold. 'Someone's bin in the night an' pinched it.'

'That's what come o' leavin' the wash on the line all night,' said Nathaniel, putting a large slice of ham into his mouth. 'I shall 'ave to buy another now, drat it.'

'But 'oo could it be?' wailed Mrs Threadgold, who was almost weeping, for she was a thrifty soul.

'Some tramp, I 'spect. Anything else missin'?'

'No, only th' shirt.'

'You're lucky then, Rose; they might ha' had the lot—your smalls an' all!'

'Ah well, some poor soul's got a shirt to 'is back; it serve me right for leavin' out the wash, I suppose.'

Meanwhile back in the workshop, Mr Threadgold's shirt was no longer recognizable as a shirt. It had been cut into wide strips and Ben and Baldmoney were busy fastening it over the framework of the Wonderbird. It was sewn on with a bone splinter needle fashioned by Ben and the thread was made of tough dried bents. Once the skeleton of the body was covered the machine began to look most workmanlike and soon the whole body was covered, save the wings. It certainly appeared very smart in its fine blue covering.

But Ben, sitting wearily back on his tail and scratching his bill with one feathery claw was doubtful. 'I don't believe it's waterproof; a shower of wet and it'll be as heavy as lead. We ought to have tested it first.'

'Well, let's test it now, before we cover the wings,' said Baldmoney. 'I'll get some water.'

He stumped out and soon reappeared with one of their little buckets full to the brim. Stepping back a pace he threw the contents all over the body and the fabric turned from bright blue to a sodden darker hue.

'Heavy as lead,' groaned Ben. 'It'll never do at all.'

'I'm afraid it won't,' said Baldmoney, glumly surveying the dripping length of the Wonderbird. 'We'd be down in the sea in no time at all.' He almost felt like weeping.

'Never mind,' said Ben cheerfully, 'it will come in useful for shirts, once a shirt always a shirt. We've got to live and learn. Before we undo all our work let's ask Yaffle. He's a wise bird and he might make a suggestion. I'll go and find him,' said Ben. 'He's sure to be up in the ash tree.'

He found Yaffle asleep in his hole up in the ash and in a very short time he was back with Ben. They found Baldmoney looking mournfully at the Wonderbird and shaking his head. The woodpecker looked all over the machine, tested the material with his bill, looked thoughtful and spoke.

'This stuff's worse than useless, but I'll go and see Kackjack, he's the bird to consult in a matter like this. I wish you'd asked me before getting the shirt; goats are always unreliable, well-meaning and all that, but no sound sense. Kackjack now, *he's* as cunning and wise as any of us, an out-and-out rascal and a bit of a thief, but I've a notion he'll find the very thing.'

'Who's Kackjack?' asked Ben. 'Do I know him?'

'Yes, I 'spect you do, he's a jackdaw who lives in the steeple of Chilcote Church over the meadows. I'll go and have a word with him.'

Yaffle found Kackjack perched on the weathercock of the steeple. He explained the whole matter to him and the jackdaw looked slyly at him out of his cunning little white eye.

'Oh ho! so the gnomes are taking to flying, are they? Whatever will they be up to next? So they want my advice, eh?'

'Yes please, Kackjack, if there's anyone who would help, it's you.'

'Mrs Bomfrey at the Red Lion has another baby— born last month,' said Kackjack, looking more sly than ever.

'I don't see what *that* has got to do with it,' said Yaffle. 'It's of no interest to us how many she has.'

'Mrs Bomfrey hangs the washing on the line every

day, yards of it and Mrs Bomfrey's babies need a lot of things.'

'Meaning?'

'Nappies, for instance, if you would know the brutal truth. Mackintosh ones.'

'Ah! Ha! Now I see your meaning,' said Yaffle admiringly. 'That sounds more like the real thing.'

'It is,' said Kackjack, 'it is. Leave it to me, Yaffle,' and the cunning rascal winked prodigiously and launched himself into space.

That evening when Ben and Baldmoney were taking a much-needed rest in the workshop, the ferns shook at the entrance and there peered in the roguish head of Kackjack. He had something in his bill: a three-cornered square of waterproof silk.

'Turns water like a duck's back,' said Kackjack, laying the material on the floor of the workshop and hopping sideways. 'I've got six more outside, shall I bring them in?'

Baldmoney took up the oiled silk and spat on it. Then he dipped it in the bucket of water and drew it out. The moisture ran off in little pearls. 'The very stuff, Kackjack, how clever you are. How did you get them?'

'Oh, it was easy. There was nobody about, I just pinched them off the line. My, but that's going to be a wonderful machine,' said the jackdaw admiringly, stepping back and half-closing one eye.

'You won't tell anyone, will you?' said Baldmoney. 'We're keeping it a dead secret and if Dodder gets to know of it he will begin to be difficult.'

''Course I won't tell,' said Kackjack, who had never

kept a secret in his life. 'But how are you going to fly it? You haven't got an engine.'

'We've thought all that out,' replied Ben. 'If you must know, I'm going to tow it. It's a glider, so it won't need an engine.'

'*Very* clever,' said the jackdaw, hopping all round the machine and trying to open one of the doors, 'very clever indeed. I might have made it myself.'

With their new material, Ben and Baldmoney worked far into the night. They ripped off Mr Threadgold's shirt and cut the waterproof silk into neat strips, sewing them tightly to the framework just as they had done the shirt. They barely stopped for a bite to eat and Mrs Ben had to do all the hunting. Towards morning, she brought her husband a mouse. Baldmoney was so excited he never ate anything at all.

In a day or so the whole machine was complete: the wings and fuselage were covered, the job was done save for a little work in the interior.

I wish you could have seen that Wonderbird because it really *was* the best thing Baldmoney had ever made. When it was finished I do believe he thought more of it than he did of the *Jeanie Deans*.

The machine was fitted with a skid at the end of each wing and one under the body, and the final touch was when Baldmoney painted the name WONDERBIRD on each side of the fuselage forward of the wings.

They made a long tow rope of plaited fibres and attached it to the nose and now it only remained to take a trial flight. It was wonderful how they had kept the secret: Dodder, Squirrel, and Sneezewort had no idea of its existence.

All the same, Dodder must have had his suspicions. Baldmoney was absent from Mr Brockett's house for hours at a stretch and he looked tired and worn and slept badly.

'I'm afraid Baldmoney's been working too hard at his Secret Plan,' Dodder confided to Squirrel one night, as they sat fishing at Windover Weir. 'Have you noticed anything?'

'Yes, I have; I believe that he and Ben are up to something. They're making another ship, I think, but I don't know for certain.'

'I'm not going to risk my bones any more,' growled Dodder. 'We could never get another ship like the *Jeanie Deans*. We're comfortable enough at Brockett's—in fact I don't see why we should move at all. The old chap seems to have taken a fancy to us and we shall be as warm as anything through the winter. Fishing's good, so why should we move at all?'

Squirrel swung in his line and re-baited the hook, and sighed.

'I'm happy enough too, up Sperrywell Lane. I'm inclined to agree with you, Dodder. I don't really think that Baldmoney and Ben are unsettled; they are never happy unless they are making things. I shouldn't let it worry you. We won't move from Sperrywell Lane, not till next spring, anyway.'

But Squirrel was wrong; their peaceful happy days were swiftly drawing to a close and the whole party was soon to be bound on a more perilous journey than they had ever dreamed of.

CHAPTER NINETEEN

The Fire at Mr Brockett's

n the last night of July, Mr Brockett, Squirrel, the gnomes, and Mr and Mrs Ben were busy playing Acorn Hop inside the badger's house. A good supper had been disposed of and the night was stormy and cold. In the fireplace the ruddy flames leapt merrily, sending strange distorted shadows from those assembled round the cheerful glow.

'I'm tired of Acorn Hop,' said Dodder, pushing the pieces off the board. 'Let's play "Ben Knows Best".'

'No, let's have a sing-song,' suggested Squirrel, 'like we used to in the old days at Rumbling Mill.'

'I'd rather someone told ghost stories,' said Sneezewort.

Baldmoney yawned. 'I'd rather have a nap.'

'You're always sleepy these days,' said Dodder. 'You

don't get enough rest. Anyway, let's put some more wood on the fire. Sneezewort, pop outside and get some more sticks.'

Grumbling, Sneezewort sulkily obeyed. Why was he always sent on errands? They kept their wood stacked close to the entrance of Mr Brockett's house. He picked his way along the sandy passages, winding in and out until he felt the cold night air blowing in upon him from the outside world.

He stood awhile listening to the sound of the wind raving in the branches of the old ash tree up above. Flying wild clouds scudded overhead and now and again he heard the eternal voice of the weir swelling and dying on the night wind.

How cosy they were down below, sitting round their bright fire! He thought he heard the far crying of curlews. These long-billed birds were never seen far inland save on the autumn migrations and these birds he heard now must have been already starting on their journeyings.

He thought of them high, so high, up there amidst the flying clouds in the wild night. Everywhere animals and birds were tucked up cosily in their various homes, the water voles and rabbits and numberless birds of every kind. Summer seemed to be running away very fast. How nice it was to think they had such a secure fortress in which to face the dread days of winter!

Shouldering a bundle, he went back down the passage, shutting the door behind him.

'What's the night like?' asked Baldmoney as Sneezewort reappeared.

'Wild and eerie, dark and dreary, and I heard some curlew a-crying.'

'They are thinking of the Autumn Flying,' said Ben. 'I know what it is, even a stay-at-home old chap like me!'

'Now, Ben, don't talk rubbish,' said Mrs Ben. 'You're too old for such nonsense.'

'Well, my dear, I used to get about a bit before I married you, and I can't help these things. It's always the same when I feel the autumn coming, I want to be up and away somewhere, over the hills and far away!'

'Don't talk like that, *please*, Ben,' said Dodder. 'Cloudberry used to carry on like that. Put some more sticks on the fire, Sneezewort.'

'Yes, yes, let's make a great big fire,' broke in Squirrel eagerly. 'It's as cold as cold tonight. Let's make the biggest fire we've *ever* made!'

So they piled on more wood and yet more wood until the vivid flames were darkened.

Then they sat in the flickering light watching the red and orange tongues lick and creep and begin to devour the mass of boughs piled above. Mr Brockett, sitting back on his couch of bracken, surveyed the happy scene. He was an animal of few words. That night he felt very happy and contented. Jolly surroundings, entertaining company, and a glorious fire to sit by—why, a few months back he would never have dreamt of such good times! To think that once he lived here all alone in the dark. Why it was a dungeon then!

Brighter grew the flames, licking and curling. Mr Brockett smiled happily. 'Tell me some more about the trip up the Folly, Dodder,' he said at last.

'But I've told it all once, twice, many times!'

'Let's hear it again, I don't mind.'

So Dodder settled himself more comfortably in the warm firelight and told all over again how they made the *Dragonfly*, how he was left behind and helped by Sir Herne, and how they came at last to the dreaded Crow Wood and met with Giant Grum.

And all the time he was retelling that immortal tale, the flames went leaping higher and higher until the heat became quite uncomfortable. Bright gold sparks fell down the chimney; more followed, then a large piece of charred wood, all glowing and sparkling, crashed down into the hearth.

Everyone jumped as though each had received an electric shock. An acrid smoke began to fill the chamber and their eyes began to smart.

'Phew!' exclaimed Baldmoney. '*What* a smeech of smoke!'

'I believe our chimney is a-fire,' said Squirrel suddenly, and just then another piece of lighted brand came crashing down. It was touch-wood from the ash above.

At that, everyone started up in alarm. Chairs were overturned and a flying spark ignited Mr Brockett's bracken bed.

In a minute it was alight and there was a mad scramble for the passage. Up the winding corridors they ran and arrived, gasping and puffing, in the open air. And there a terrible spectacle met their affrighted gaze. The old touch-wood ash tree was spouting a mass of fire like some huge engine chimney. Gold sparks were flying upwards, it seemed as if the very bowels of the earth were gushing fire.

It was a good thing that nobody was in the room below. This was now a seething mass of flame and billows of choking smoke began to waver up through the doorway. Not a living thing could exist down there; they had escaped in the nick of time.

Poor old Mr Brockett was aghast. The glow of the fire, the reflection of the flames on the dense clouds of oily smoke, truly presented an awesome sight. Other animals began to gather around, their eyeballs glinting in the hellish blaze, rabbits, hedge-pigs, and affrighted birds.

Everyone was talking at once. Someone suggested that the gnomes should try and put out the fire by water but their little pails held so little.

Meanwhile, down below, in Mr Brockett's house, the hungry flames crept along the sandy walls. Cupboards and sideboards, chairs and tables, made with so much care by Baldmoney, became alight, one after the other, and greenish choking smoke came forth from the door like poisonous gases.

Mr Brockett was distracted. Why had he ever let the gnomes build a fireplace in his house? Why had he ever taken them in! Now his house was ruined, he would never get rid of the smell of burning, even when the tree had burnt itself out!

By now the conflagration had begun to attract attention from other people beside animals and birds. Mrs Threadgold, who was letting the cat out for the night, saw the dull leaping glow on the far side of the river and against it were silhouetted the branches of the pollard willows by the weir. She ran back to Mr Threadgold, who was smoking his pipe by the kitchen fire.

'Nathaniel! Nathaniel! There's summat afire up at Sperrywell Lane, looks like a rick or summat, there ain't no house that way, be there?'

'P'raps it's an airyplane a-burnin',' said Mr Threadgold,

hastily slipping his feet into his carpet slippers and shuffling to the door. From the threshold of the cottage they could now see bright tongues of fire peeping and winking above the thick bushes of the lane.

Farmers and others, attracted by the flames, were already making their way across the fields and of course at their coming the animals made themselves scarce. The gnomes and their friends, hurrying down the lane to find some shelter, almost ran into a party of labourers who had crossed the river by Windover Cottage. They crouched under a bramble bush while the men went by and heard them talking among themselves.

'It's th'ole touch-wood ash,' said one.

'An' a fine old blaze he do make,' said another.

Then came Farmer Goosegrass from Chilcote Farm with a watercart and soon gallons and gallons of water were cascading down into Mr Brockett's dwelling. The burning wood hissed and sizzled and soon the underground house was full of water; you never saw such a mess in all your life.

It was well after midnight before the flames were put out and weary men were able to return to their homes, marvelling one with another how the fire had started.

And when Mr Brockett and the gnomes came to inspect the damage, it was truly appalling. Water stood inches deep in the main living-room and everywhere there was the ghastly smell of wet charred wood. To think of living there now was quite impossible. What worried the gnomes was that all their treasures had been consumed in the fire: their spare clothes, the Acorn Hop board, everything but what they stood up in.

What worried Mr Brockett was that there was no other

suitable sett (which is the name for a badger's house) in Sperrywell Lane and it takes years to dig a really good roomy place. The only thing for him to do was to move to another disused sett in a quarry over beyond Chilcote village, and that was not nearly so safe as that in Sperrywell Lane, there were too many keepers there. But it was the only place.

Poor old Mr Brockett, it *was* hard lines on him, and the gnomes really felt very sorry for him because they had been the cause of the whole catastrophe.

'No more fires for me, thank you,' said the old badger grimly, as he surveyed the ruins of his home. 'I don't mind you living with me but I won't have anything to do with that stuff. You can come with me to Chilcote Park if you like, but mind—no fires!'

Dodder drew Baldmoney aside.

'This is going to be difficult,' he said. 'We *must* have a fire, we've always been used to it, we can't go and live with him. We must find some other place!'

Poor little men, one cannot help feeling sorry for them, as well as for Mr Brockett. It was the third time their home had been broken up. 'I don't know what we shall do or where we shall go.'

Ben nudged Baldmoney and whispered something in his ear. Baldmoney cleared his throat.

'Look, Dodder, Ben and I have something to tell you. We don't have to find another home, not here anyway. The only place where we shall find any peace is Woodcock's island.'

'What's that you say?' gasped Dodder, wiping his grimy face with his sleeve. '*Woodcock's island!* But that's far away and we can't get there now we've lost our ship!'

'Oh yes we can, if you promise not to be difficult. Ben and I have been working for weeks on our Plan and it's finished now. Come and look at it.'

Rather heartlessly leaving Mr Brockett to survey the ruins of his home, Baldmoney led the way down the lane and pushing aside the ferns ushered Dodder into the workshop.

As soon as the latter caught sight of the Wonderbird, he stopped short. 'But you told me it wasn't a thunderbird; I *won't* go in a thunderbird!'

'It isn't a *proper* thunderbird,' said Ben gently, 'it's a glider and I'm going to tow it. There's room inside for everybody, including Squirrel and we believe it will be the means of quitting this country for ever and taking us safe and sound across the Irish Sea.'

'Look inside,' wheedled Baldmoney, knowing full well the latter's weakness for cunning woodwork. 'See if it isn't the most comfortable machine that's ever been made. Here, try this chair, we've made it for you so you can look out of the window.'

Dodder sat down in the little reed chair. It certainly *was* very comfortable, as comfortable as the *Jeanie Deans*. He looked along inside the plane and saw how neatly everything had been fitted up with little lockers and cupboards; even a little closet in the tail of the plane.

'Um ha, it certainly is a nice looking bit of work, but how do you know it will fly?'

'We are sure it will fly. Ben says so and Ben knows best.'

'Um,' said Dodder, still looking very doubtful. 'Well, I might as well break my old bones in this as in anything, I suppose.'

'And we'll try it out tomorrow,' exclaimed Baldmoney, feeling a rush of thankfulness that Dodder had taken it so well. 'Of course, if it won't fly that's that, and we'll have to stay, but if it does as we think it will, will you come to Woodcock's island?'

Dodder, sitting back in his little chair, and gazing around him with an admiration he could not disguise, nodded his head.

Meanwhile, Sneezewort and Squirrel, covered as they were in smuts and smelling of wood-smoke, were inspecting every inch of the Wonderbird, both inside and out. They poked their noses into the cupboards, they inspected a very beautifully drawn chart which Baldmoney had made of their coming journey (he had got all the details from Woodcock long ago) and Sneezewort was especially intrigued with the little lockers by each seat. These were let into the wall of the plane and were of course only a few inches deep. He pushed aside a little sliding panel and there was a neat package, three inches by three, wrapped in oiled silk.

'What's this, Baldmoney?'

The inventor, with a proud smile, undid the package. 'Parachute; Ben says we must all have parachutes, and he helped me make 'em.'

'What's a parachute?'

'Fancy not knowing what a parachute is! Why, it's a little umbrella, rather like the ladybirds have, and you strap it on your back and if anything happens to the plane—as of course it won't—then you can jump out and float down to the ground in safety.'

'And supposing you are over the sea?' asked Sneezewort.

'Well, the same thing happens—how silly you are,

Sneezewort!—and anyway we shan't have to use them. For Pan's sake, don't mention them to Dodder or he'll get scared and think that the Wonderbird isn't safe!'

While Baldmoney had been showing Sneezewort the parachutes—which I forgot to mention were made of Mr Threadgold's shirt, which had come in useful after all— Squirrel was examining the windows. These were made from little squares of celluloid. Kackjack had produced a quantity of it from the garage dump in Chilcote village. It had originally formed the back panel to an old Morris car. Only Baldmoney could have fitted those windows so neatly and efficiently. There was an emergency exit at the back of the plane and over each bucket seat was a tiny rack to hold odds and ends. Originally there had been many other gadgets but Ben had persuaded, nay insisted, that they should all be taken out again. All down the centre of the roof were little fibre slings such as one sees in an underground train. These were of course in case passengers should want to go and wash their hands in the closet at the back.

After making a final inspection of the Wonderbird, everyone lay down on the floor of the workshop and had a sleep. They had been through a great deal in the last few hours; the reek of the fire was still about their clothes and all were unspeakably dirty. But washing would have to come later. Ben, whose tail feathers had been singed, looked a sorry sight, but the fact that Dodder had proved so amenable over the Wonderbird compensated for a lot and, quite worn out, everyone was soon fast asleep.

Not so poor old Mr Brockett. He snuffed and grunted about the ruins of his house and twice he tried to penetrate to the inner room, but the smell and dirt and water drove him back. Moreover he felt hurt that the others had forsaken him in his hour of distress; the earth seemed to have swallowed them up. And feeling extremely put out and wishing he had never set eyes on the gnomes, he at last took himself off to Chilcote Park just as grey dawn was setting every farmyard cock a-tiptoe. Faint wisps of steam still curled up from the interior of the ash stump which was now no more than a blackened hollow shell and on an oak close by an astonished Yaffle was gazing at the night's work, wondering what on earth had happened. He had slept through the whole drama and had never even smelt the fire, or heard a sound!

CHAPTER TWENTY

Wonderbird Tries Her Wings

 can make no excuses for the treatment meted out to Mr Brockett, I hold no brief for the gnomes, Bens, nor Squirrel. I can only think that it was a case of sheer thoughtlessness on their part, such as children are wont to display at times in their relations to their elders.

The fact that it was entirely due to their 'modern improvements' that Mr Brockett's house had gone up (or down) in flames, did not occur to them, and they thought no more about it. Of course, it was not surprising. Their heads were full of the Wonderbird and her coming trial flight; in fact, the tense atmosphere was very similar to that time immediately prior to the launching of the *Dragonfly* in the far-off Folly days.

The morning following the fire dawned bright and fair. The sun shone and not a cloud was to be seen in the whole ocean of sky. But to risk a flight in broad day was not advisable, because Windover Weir was, as I have said before, by no means a lonely spot; indeed, now that August Bank Holiday was so close, it was to be expected that there would be many picnic parties in the water-meadows all about.

So all that lovely day the gnomes and Squirrel had to fret and pace up and down in the shadow of the ferns and undergrowth waiting impatiently for evening to cast its mantle upon the river valley.

The Bens were wiser: they spent the hours of light in Chilcote Church tower, a very owly, ratty place. Kackjack met them there and he would keep the two birds awake by talking and chattering until Ben had to shut him up. 'How can we get any sleep if you are going to chatter, chatter, chatter, from hour to hour the way you do? Don't you know that we want to try out our Wonderbird tonight and how can we be fresh and have our wits about us if we get no sleep?'

And Kackjack was very rude and said that if it hadn't been for him (Kackjack) they wouldn't have been able to finish the Wonderbird at all. But the wise Bens held their peace and Kackjack soon got tired and popped out of the lancet louvres of the tower and left them to a quiet nap.

How musty it was within the tower, how very old it smelt—like a cave! For company they had numerous spiders and bats. Ropes, massive wheels, and mighty bells hung silent and moveless, but the church clock kept measure of the dusty hours with a solemn 'Tick! tock! Tick! tock!' This sound had been the lullaby for countless

Kackjack babies and owlets too. And as the sunbeams wheeled gradually across the uneven floor of the belfry (in those rays were suspended millions of dust particles so that they seemed solid bars) the clock woke up each hour, whirrings started from some hidden source and the echoing sombre tones went rolling forth across the quiet churchyard with its yews and unclipped graves.

At last, when the drowsy sun of that late summer afternoon had described a half-circuit of the floor, and when the bands of martins and swallows had ceased to twitter and hawk about the tower and had taken themselves off to the telephone wires outside the Red Lion, the Bens awoke and rubbed their bills, blinked and blinked again, and wondered where they were. Of course—the Wonderbird! The Wonderbird was to have her trial flight that very evening! They shook their feathers, which still smelt of wood-smoke, and Mrs Ben tried to tidy up her husband for his tail was very singed.

Then they kissed each other, by locking their bills like pigeons do, popped through a broken slat in the lancet and glided away towards Sperrywell Lane. They found as much excitement there as when the *Dragonfly* set sail from Oak Tree House, or the *Jeanie Deans* from Rumbling Mill. Dodder was a bit annoyed but Baldmoney felt extremely important. And at the last moment who should turn up but that vulgar Kackjack! The vain bird strutted about telling the crowd that he had made the Wonderbird, but nobody believed him.

At last, when the sun sank behind the tall poplars by Windover Weir and the river gleamed like a metal blade in the last of the light, Dodder cleared a way through the spectators and formed them in a wide semicircle in the lane. Rabbits and hedge-pigs were in the majority and at the last moment Ben thought of the goats and knew how upset they would be to miss the fun. So they sent Sneezewort and Squirrel across to the orchard to untie them and very soon the old he-goat and his nanny and two kids came bounding like stags up the lane, all their tails straight up in the air like startled deers'.

Baldmoney had made a little wooden trolley and with the help of the others they lifted the Wonderbird aboard it. She was wonderfully light, thanks to Ben's minute instructions. And then they pulled it up the lane in the twilight and all the animals and birds came crowding after, talking excitedly.

Ben had found a suitable place for the launching: it was from a steep little bank at the top of Sperrywell Lane. It faced the river valley and the grass was short and fine, nibbled by generations of rabbits.

Twilight was deepening into night when the great moment drew near and the whole river valley was cloaked in a white mist. Not a breath of wind was blowing and the only sound in the tranquil air was the low talk of Windover Weir in the distance. The hum of the crowd had been hushed into a tense expectancy, everyone spoke in whispers.

A bramble rustled in the ditch and for a moment rabbits and birds were poised for flight. But it was only Mr Brockett. He came lumbering out of the ditch with never a word, and the gnomes and Squirrel felt very awkward and ashamed. They had not even let him know about the launching of the Wonderbird! But the old fellow, by some strange inner vision, felt something unusual was going on at Sperrywell Lane and so had come to see for himself.

Squirrel arranged the tow rope in a cunning bridle around Ben's shoulders and with a gay wave of his hand Baldmoney climbed into the body of the machine. Inwardly he was quaking with fear and excitement, outwardly he was the bold aviator about to set out on some record-breaking flight.

He made his way forward to the cockpit and felt for the joy-stick which controlled the plane. Many weeks of coaching by Ben had given him a very good idea of how to fly the Wonderbird and now he was glad to find his head clear and senses keyed up; he remembered everything he had been told.

'Good luck,' Dodder shouted up at the little window where they could just see the top of Baldmoney's skin cap.

Squirrel, standing well out on the grass in front of Ben, dropped his paw, which was the signal for Ben to get under way. The owl ran along the ground as fast as he could and Sneezewort and Dodder pushed the Wonderbird from behind.

On the smooth grass her skids ran easily. Faster, faster they went for the brow of the hill and at last Ben opened his spotted wings and beat along like a swan trying to leave the water into a head wind.

The Wonderbird rocked a little, her wings dipped this way and that, just touching the grass. Ben was now airborne, the rope became taut, and the next instant the Wonderbird was airborne too, rising gracefully into the air and keeping an even trim.

Up, up they went, old Ben flogging away in front, the graceful Wonderbird following behind, out, out of the river mists, until they were lost to view! A subdued cheer went up from those assembled round about and soon everyone was babbling excitedly one to another.

And in a little while eager eyes made out the form of Ben, still towing the glider, heading in from the direction of Chilcote. They passed right overhead at a height of fifty feet or more, turned and came back. The tow dropped, Ben did a quick turn and came to rest on a gate post and the Wonderbird, turning gracefully again, came gliding in to make a perfect landing on the grass, scattering the rabbits and birds right and left. Only one accident occurred and that was to a hedge-pig, who was struck on the nose by one of the wing skids. He rolled over and over but picked himself up none the worse.

Then the door flew open and Baldmoney stepped out, grinning all over his little red face.

'Bravo! Bravo!' said everyone. 'Well done, Baldmoney! Well done!'

'There's nothing much wrong with her,' said Baldmoney, blowing on his hands. 'The only thing was it was jolly cold up there. We shall have to make some extra thick coats and gloves. But as for the plane, she couldn't be better!'

'Three cheers for Baldmoney and the gnomes!' shouted an excited otter who, unknown to anyone, had come up from the river to see what all the to-do was about. 'Three cheers for the clever air-gnomes!'

But Baldmoney took Ben by the shoulder and thrust him forward. 'Here is the real hero, souls,' he cried. 'Ben is the one to deserve your cheers, Ben knows best!'

And every animal and bird took up the cry amidst great laughter. 'Ben Knows Best! Ben Knows Best!' and the cries echoed around the little hill.

Poor old Ben was so confused he didn't know which way to look.

Of course, the birds were the most interested spectators. They hopped on the wings and peeped into the cabin and discussed all the fine points of the Wonderbird.

Soon Dodder had to act as policeman, and waving his stick he headed them off, for Baldmoney feared the Wonderbird might be damaged, and you never know to what length souvenir hunters will go and there were several kackjacks in the crowd, as sly as sly.

Now the flight was over and the Wonderbird had proved her paces she was lifted back on to the trolley and a little after midnight was safely back again in the workshop down Sperrywell Lane. Everyone felt very happy and pleased, especially Ben and Baldmoney, who had worked and planned for so long. It was indeed a sweet hour of triumph for them.

And best of all, Dodder was as excited as any, and thought that the Wonderbird was the finest thing they had ever built! And I am glad to say they showed some civility to poor old Mr Brockett and instead of allowing him to go back to Chilcote Park, they persuaded him to stay the night with them in the workshop. The gnomes said how sorry they were they had ever suggested building a chimney in his precious sett. The badger took it all very well and everyone was happy, I am glad to say, and though they would have liked to take Badger with them in the plane, of course that was *quite* out of the question!

CHAPTER TWENTY-ONE

Airborne

or the two days following the trials of Wonderbird, the gnomes set to work to make extra flying equipment. The Bens hunted as they had never done before and brought them mole and mouse skins and the little men stitched and stitched all day long and half the night.

They made thick fur gloves and helmets, and warm duffle coats, and even fur boots. Even then they found time to collect together a store of food to take with then on the journey. Squirrel made a completely new set of fishing gear and Yaffle seemed very busy also and they saw little of him.

At last all was ready and one evening a crowd again assembled on the flying field at the top of Sperrywell Lane, only this time an even larger number of animals and birds were gathered together. They meant to give the gnomes a grand send-off. And early in the evening who should appear but two of the otters from Rumbling Mill *and* the King of Fishers, *and* dear old Watervole!

How they had got to know beats me, but, as I said before, news spreads quickly in the wilds. It must have meant a very long journey for their old friends from Rumbling Mill. It was all very touching, especially as time was so short, and the gnomes had barely a moment to greet their well-loved comrades. Each and all had so much to tell but alas! there was no time for talk, not even time for an Animal Banquet. I think Mr Brockett was very impressed to see how many friends the gnomes had made. He never realized their popularity and how distinguished were his erstwhile guests.

It was a perfect night for the take-off. A gentle breeze was blowing from the west right on to the top of the hill. The Wonderbird had never looked so trim and workmanlike. Squirrel went round her and examined the skids and tested them, Baldmoney tested the controls, and Sneezewort went round her with a duster, removing invisible specks of dirt from her sides and wings. And of course, just before the take-off, a starling must needs make a mess on one of the wings! The poor bird did not mean to, it was sheer excitement. But it had to be washed off and Baldmoney was fuming to be off.

'I can't believe you are *really* going to leave us and this island of ours,' said the King of Fishers. 'I only hope you will find the fishing as good on Woodcock's island!'

'Think of us sometimes,' cried the Otters from Rumbling Mill. 'Give a thought to us back here in the old country!'

'Don't forget the old days by the Folly,' squeaked Watervole. 'Pan keep you, give you an easy journey and bring you back again safe and sound!'

Baldmoney climbed aboard first, putting on his new fur gloves in a professional manner and giving a jaunty wave to the assembled multitude. Then followed Dodder (he had to be helped up into the plane by Sneezewort), then came Squirrel, carrying a bag of nuts in his teeth, and finally Sneezewort, who raised both thumbs at the crowd. The door was shut-to and Ben, who all this time had been looking over his shoulder like a restive greyhound, settled himself grimly into the towing harness.

Just at that moment a breathless Yaffle appeared with swift and dipping flight over the bushes. He was carrying something square in his bill. He came breathlessly through the crowd and lo and behold, he presented Sneezewort with a new Acorn Hop Board, which he had made all himself!

The door of the plane shut-to again and now the heads of Dodder and Baldmoney could be seen peering out of the windows, laughing and nodding and waving their hands.

First Mrs Ben took off in front, then Ben put down his head and charged like a bull along the hilltop. The tow rope dipped and tightened and the Wonderbird began to move swiftly forward over the grass.

Breathless, the crowd watched, never a sound was heard as the glider left the ground and then a great cheer went up, the animals waved, the birds flew hither and thither over and above the moving plane.

Away they went, out over the valley, dwindling smaller and smaller, heading for the last glow of the sunset sky.

'I can still see them!' squeaked a field vole, dancing up and down on tiptoes. 'Goodbye! Goodbye!' shouted the

Rumbling Mill Otters, and then, when the two tiny specks melted into the infinite distance, the crowd dispersed their several ways, feeling life was very tame for stay-at-homes. Soon the little hill was empty, save for one lonely and wistful figure—poor old Mr Brockett. Tears were running down his furry cheeks, he sat hunched like a sick bear, his striped head sunk in his shoulders. I think he was more cut up than anyone. He had tasted a few short weeks of utter bliss, weeks which had been even worth the fire!

Baldmoney at the controls had hardly time to glance out of the windows. His eyes were on the tow rope and the flying shape of Ben. The old owl was flying with slow and measured beats and ahead, acting as pilot, was Mrs Ben.

Dodder and Squirrel, who had good seats, both with windows, gazed down like Lords on the landscape below. They saw the steeple of Chilcote Church swim under; they looked down into the tops of the rounded elms and neat cottage gardens, all very dim in the gathering darkness.

In a short while, a matter of minutes, the village and river had been left behind. They did not catch a glimpse of the goats because of the apple-trees. The poor beasts had been unable to attend the final send-off.

Woods and parklands, mansions and hamlets, ponds and streams, all passed below in slow succession. The ponds, reflecting the last light in the sky, shone like crystals, the rivers and streams as silver threads.

Ben was climbing. Baldmoney, his eyes on the chart and on his instrument panel (it was too dark to see Ben now) felt exultant. How smoothly the plane rode the air! There was no thump of screw nor jarring of machinery, only faint squeaks in the framework and the low hiss of the wind about the windows.

Poor Sneezewort was in the dark interior at the back; he could see nothing but the portly back of Squirrel and a bit of Dodder's fur cap.

Making the most of his opportunities he slyly opened one of the cupboards close behind him but was disgusted to find only spare clothing. He tried another which he was sure contained food, but it was locked. The cunning Baldmoney had seen to that.

Dodder leant back in his seat and sighed, half in relief and half in sorrow.

'Well, it was a grand send-off, Squirrel.'

'Yes indeed, the best we've ever had.'

'But it's sad saying goodbye. I *hate* goodbyes!'

'So do I,' replied Squirrel heartily. 'That's the worst of making friends.'

'Where are we now, Baldmoney?' asked Dodder, trying to peep over the pilot's shoulder.

'Getting near the sea, I should say. Keep a look-out for it, any minute now!'

The moon was rising and very soon they saw the land below grow dark and then lines of white appeared. They were the breakers beating on a lonely beach.

The gnomes had never seen the sea, nor had Squirrel; the spectacle was awe-inspiring. Soon the land was left behind and beneath them was nothing but sea, which looked as solid as the land. A ship was visible here and there, very small and far-away, trailing a long streamer of white behind it like a snail on a garden path.

And then veils of moonlit cloud began to hide the void beneath, massed woolly blankets hid everything and they seemed to be flying through an unreal dream-world. Ahead of the Wonderbird the Bens were now invisible, flying with measured beats. And soon (thrilling sight!) they passed a flock of birds, they knew not what, flying in the same direction as themselves.

Dodder poked Squirrel and pointed, but at that moment the fog hid them from view.

More cloud and yet more clouds swam by, over them sometimes, veiling the forms of the Bens. It was eerie for Baldmoney, sitting forward in his pilot's seat, to see the tow-rope disappearing into nothingness ahead, and to feel the invisible agency gently towing them along.

Occasionally they felt the jar of a wind pocket, the plane lurched and dropped a foot or so, and Baldmoney felt his heart jump into his throat. The sensation was very like that of a boy who is flying a kite in a high wind who feels the line slacken and then pull taut again.

The whitish clouds grew more sombre and soon they seemed to dive into a blackness as of moonless night. Sharp raps smote the windows and the sides of the Wonderbird. It was rain. Ben, out in front, began to be a little weary. They were heading straight into the storm, and his feathers began to feel heavy, the tow rope to chafe his shoulders.

But in a moment or so they were through the cloud and, once more, there was the shining limitless sea all green and grey, and crinkled in the moonlight, while overhead the stars shone bright and clear.

It was a wondrous spectacle to the intrepid air-gnomes. It was certainly the most thrilling adventure they ever had. No wonder Cloudberry had enjoyed his trip with the Heaven Hounds, if it was anything like this! And they could enjoy it more in the cosy security of the Wonderbird.

What a clever fellow was Baldmoney, thought Dodder, as he sat back in his comfortable chair, he really *was*. To think he could build such a Wonderbird!

'We'll be sighting the Irish coast soon,' called the pilot over his shoulder.

'You don't say so!' exclaimed Dodder. 'D'you really mean that?'

'Yes, according to my chart we should, in the next hour at any rate!'

The lulling action of the glider made Dodder almost drowsy. He would awake with a start and wonder where he was and then smile happily when he knew.

Now a subtle change began to take place. Instead of the moonlit sea they saw a faint whitish vapour which grew more and more dense as they progressed. It looked exactly like a snow-covered landscape except there was nothing to break the monotony of the expanse—no tree, no hedge, nor wood.

'Fog,' muttered Baldmoney, drawing in his breath. 'I expect Ben will try and get below it.'

Almost at once, the tow rope began to slant downwards. Cunning bird! He was going down through the fog to get his bearings! The gnomes felt a little queer as they began to drop down towards that woolly blanket and for the first time they felt an insecure feeling in the pits of their stomachs.

It was rather like going down in a lift. Then the luminous vapour arose and engulfed them and they could not see a thing. Thicker it grew and thicker, but still they flew on into nothingness.

'Don't like this fog,' said Baldmoney, looking very grave. 'Just our luck to choose a foggy night. But don't let's worry, Ben will see us through.'

In actual fact, Ben was getting very tired. The constant strain of the tow-rope bridle about his shoulders and the impenetrable fog was worrying him a lot. He went down and down, lower and lower; but still he could see nothing. Was there land beneath or sea? How could he tell?

And as he dropped he heard a sound—the uneasy chafe and sullen splash of waves. They were almost in the sea! Out of the murk arose a hungry foam-flecked roller which sank again from sight.

Sharply he pulled up.

The sudden slackening of the tow rope made Baldmoney almost sick with fear. But the thorough training he had received from Ben stood him in good stead.

He pulled back the joystick and the Wonderbird answered at once. They swept upward again in a graceful glide. Beads of perspiration glistened on his brow. Meanwhile, in the rear, Dodder had been thrown violently forward and Squirrel seemed to be hanging round his neck. Sneezewort was upside down in the rear of the plane, gasping and puffing.

'Phew!' said Baldmoney. 'That was a near thing; we nearly hit the sea!'

'Please be careful,' piped Dodder faintly. 'Don't try any of those tricks again.'

'Better be on the safe side and put on your parachutes,' retorted Baldmoney. 'With this fog anything might happen. I'm doing my best, I can't do more.'

All the gnomes had been taught how to put them on

by Ben and they were accordingly adjusted. Squirrel's of course was bigger than the others but it worked on the same principle. Once these were fixed I think everyone felt a little safer. Baldmoney had some difficulty in putting on his but with the help of Dodder, they managed it.

'We should have put them on before we started,' puffed Baldmoney, red in the face with the exertion, 'but in the hurry and bustle I forgot.'

'I hope we don't have to use them,' said Dodder nervously.

Meanwhile poor Ben was becoming very weary indeed. They had gained altitude but the effort had been very exhausting and the fog showed no signs of lifting. The journey which had begun so well and with so much promise was now rather like a bad dream to all concerned. But bravely Ben flew on into the gloom, hoping for the best and the chance of the fog lifting. After a while things seemed to be a little easier. Whether Ben got his second wind I do not know, but he certainly felt stronger and everyone felt more confident. After all, they were not doing so badly, considering!

Dodder began to doze again and then he felt a craving for his pipe. He pulled it out, filled and lit it, and the blue clouds of fragrant weed filled the interior of the Wonderbird. Now and again Squirrel or Dodder would pull back the window and peer out, but the cold wind soon made them slide the window to again. They were very glad of their warm coats.

Baldmoney looked keenly at the chart. 'Must be over the land now surely,' he said to himself, and then aloud, 'We ought to have reached the coast ten minutes ago!'

'There's no telling,' said Dodder, knocking out his pipe. 'With this fog we can't see a yard, nor can Ben.'

The stuffy atmosphere of the cabin, due to the tight-shut windows, made Dodder begin to nod again. He must have fallen asleep because the next thing he remembered was Squirrel shaking him violently by the arm. 'Dodder! Dodder! Something's burning!'

Dodder was awake in a moment and Baldmoney, screwing half-round in his seat, sniffed the air. Something was indeed burning! They seemed haunted by fire! And it wasn't tobacco—*it was the Wonderbird.*

A spark from Dodder's pipe which had fallen unnoticed under his bucket seat had set fire to the floor and the horrified gnomes and Squirrel, looking down, saw the oiled silk was well alight. What a terrible moment! What a terrible death confronted them! And quite unconscious of it all the gallant Ben was plodding ahead in the fog and thinking how well they were getting along!

Now at this crucial moment only a clear head and a calm nerve could have saved them all from certain death. It is in such moments that the best in a man or a gnome becomes evident and Baldmoney was no longer Leader of the Ship. It was Dodder—Dodder, who many months before, had saved Sneezewort from the jaws of the Wood Dog up the Folly.

'We shall have to jump,' he said in a quiet voice. 'In a minute or two the whole thing will be alight. Sneezewort, is your parachute fastened properly?'

Sneezewort, ashen of face, could only nod. Baldmoney started up from the controls and clambered over Dodder. There was danger of a sudden panic which would have been fatal, and the Wonderbird, with no one at the controls, lurched and plunged sideways dragging Ben head-over-heels.

Luckily the towing bridle came adrift from the startled and unhappy bird and the next moment he saw the glider plunging like a flaming torch towards the earth or sea.

But as it fell, first one small figure, then another, dropped from it. First fell Baldmoney, then Sneezewort, then Squirrel, who was emitting thin and threadlike squeaks of terror, then Dodder, and as they hurtled through space Ben saw a puff of material above each falling victim and heaved a sigh of relief. At any rate the parachutes *had* opened and all four of his friends were drifting and floating gently down in the fog.

The firebrand which had once been the Wonderbird, was no longer a bird of wonder but of horror. It plunged meteor-like into the murk, becoming, after a second or two, a mere dull illumination in the horrid vapour of night and finally vanished from Ben's gaze.

Down, down, the gnomes and Squirrel floated, swinging slightly from side to side. Those first few awful moments had been the worst, when they felt themselves drawn by the pull of earth. But now it was extraordinarily restful, sinking down so gently in the clammy mist. Each had lost sight of the other, each felt absolutely alone and forsaken, yet there was a serene sense of peace and soft motion.

Dodder, swinging like a spider from a thread, looked up and saw above him the billowing bowl of Mr Threadgold's shirt. Wonderful shirt! Glorious shirt! A shirt destined for the final drama which was now being enacted!

The crying of birds passed him and he heard the rustle of wings. This surely was the end of all their earthly adventures! Strange years, strange years—Cuckoo Years they had called them—when they lived in such peace and quiet in the old Oak Tree. Uneasy years, when Cloudberry left them and then, passing before his mind, he saw again the *Jeanie Deans* reposing on the sand at Poplar Island, and the journey and homecoming amid the snow to the safe haven of the Oak Tree and Cloudberry standing smiling there!

Happy months at Rumbling Mill! Happy times with Mr Brockett! And now this was the end!

But see—what was that wondrous illumination directly below which grew brighter every moment until it seemed to fill the world. Was he falling into the sun?

And as he fell this light was shut out as if by a moving blind—to appear and grow again with an even greater intensity until Dodder was quite dazzled with its glory. At that moment his leg struck something hard, he felt a terrific blow on his chest, and then all was a darkness as profound and silent as the deepest night!

CHAPTER TWENTY-TWO

At the Knockgobbin Light

 onsciousness for Dodder began as a slowly growing radiance and a low soothing surge of watery sounds and many birds' voices.

As the seconds passed, all his faculties gradually returned. He found that he was lying on some sort of hard surface, his face turned towards the sky, while overhead that blinding light, which seemed brighter than the sun in all his splendour, alternately lightened and darkened.

Feebly he moved his arms and his one good leg. About him was tangled the harness of his parachute, the blue shirt almost enveloped him. Where was he? What had happened? Then he lay quite still trying to piece together his thoughts. Bit by bit the events of the last few hours fitted in; he remembered the start from the Flying Field, the sad farewells, the sight of the dusky landscape passing below. Ah! now he knew—the Wonderbird had caught fire, they had jumped for their lives, and now here he was lying in a queer place, the like of which he had never seen before.

This blinding light which swelled and faded, the continual twitter and chatter of sweet bird voices above him and from all sides—was this the Gnomes' Heaven? Certainly the bird music suggested it. And as at last he felt his strength returning he sat up, freeing himself from the enveloping ropes and tangle of his parachute.

Immediately above his head was a vast iron grill behind which the light swung, and perched on the wires and along the railings close by were hundreds and hundreds of birds, all chattering excitedly. Their wings filled the air; some hovered and clung to the grill like moths fascinated by a candle, others fell down, dazed and exhausted, on the platform where Dodder lay.

After a while he was aware that a very small voice was making itself heard in his left ear, and turning his head he saw close beside him a common house-mouse. It had not the refined accent of a dormouse or hedge-vole, it dropped its aitches, so to speak, but it talked in a delightful brogue which reminded Dodder of Woodcock.

'Sure, but it's a woeful knock you've had and a bruise on your head as big as a cherry. But lie still where you are, and soon ye will be better.'

'Where am I, House-mouse?' groaned Dodder, relieved beyond measure that here at last was someone to talk to.

'Faith, but it's the Knockgobbin Light where ye are, and fancy you not knowing it! How did you come here, seeing as you have no wings like the birds?'

'We came in the Wonderbird—a glider you know—

and it caught fire, and we all had to jump with our parachutes and then—I don't know what happened.'

Suddenly the house-mouse let out a squeak of fear. 'Och! is it two owls I see on the top of the Light yonder?'

'They won't harm you,' cried Dodder, staggering to his feet. (Oh blessed birds, so they had not deserted him.) 'They won't touch you—' The mouse was trying to hide under Dodder's parachute. '—it's only the Bens, they won't harm any of my friends.'

'I'll not be trusting them,' whimpered the mouse. 'I'll be away to my hole.'

'Don't run away, House-mouse, I tell you they won't harm a hair of your head. Hi, Bens! Bens! Come down here . . . It's Dodder and there's a friend of mine with me—House-mouse—who's afraid of you!'

Down swooped the two birds, alighting on the rail close beside them.

'Ben! Ben!' cried Dodder, laying his hand on the shoulder of his old friend. He noticed the feathers had been worn away all round the owl's neck, so that the wrinkled yellow skin showed. 'How *glad* I am to see you both. This is House-mouse—or should I say Lighthouse-mouse?' said Dodder correcting himself. He introduced the little creature, who was trembling visibly.

The Bens bowed in a courtly fashion and set him at his ease.

'Lighthouse-mouse tells me we're at Knockgobbin Light.'

'Is this the Knockgobbin Light?' gasped Ben. 'Then we've reached Woodcock's island after all!'

'But where is Squirrel and the others?' said Dodder. 'Don't say they've gone, don't say you haven't seen them!'

Here the mouse piped up. 'Please, if you mean another gnome and a squirrel, they are farther along the gallery, I saw them as I came along.'

'Let's go and find them,' gasped Ben, 'and see if they are all right and no broken bones. *What* a crowd,' said the owl as he shouldered a passage through the thronging birds.

'It's the night of the Autumn Flying,' squeaked Lighthouse-mouse, as they hurried along close behind Ben, 'they've been arriving since the fog came down; we get all sorts of folk on the night of the Autumn Flying.'

Ben, leading the way, tripped over an exhausted housemartin. 'Beg pardon, I didn't see you,' said the kind old owl, helping it to its feet. The little bird was too scared to reply but lay cowering at the foot of the great lantern. All it could say was 'Oh! Oh!'

Before very long, as they elbowed their way through the press of birds, all of whom had the appearance of a large multitude of very weary travellers at some great terminus, Ben caught sight of Squirrel. The tired animal was leaning against the railings gingerly feeling with his paw a large lump, as big as a hedge-sparrow's egg, over his right eye. And Sneezewort, with the complete back missing from his skin pants, was busy making a bandage out of a scrap of rag. They did not hear or see the approach of the Bens and Dodder. Squirrel was moaning 'Oh! my poor head! Oh! my poor head!' and Sneezewort, who seemed little the worse, was trying to comfort him.

'Cheer up, Squirrel old man, you'll soon be yourself again, we're lucky to be alive if you ask me. I expect poor old Dodder and Baldmoney have been smashed to pieces or drowned.'

Dodder brought his hand down on Sneezewort's shoulder.

'Dodder!'

'Sneezewort!'

'Dodder, *and* the Bens too, if I'm not dreaming. Look, Squirrel, who's here!'

Squirrel seemed to forget all his troubles. He hugged Dodder and then the Bens and so joyful was the reunion that quite a ring of interested birds formed round them.

Meanwhile Lighthouse-mouse was hanging back, watching it all; feeling, for the moment, rather out of the picture.

'But where is Baldmoney!' exclaimed Squirrel. 'Isn't he with you?'

The gnomes looked anxiously about.

'Haven't seen a sign of him,' said Sneezewort, 'but he may be in the crowd somewhere.'

'Yes, he may,' said Dodder hopefully. 'It's hard to tell with all these people.'

'Where *have* all these birds come from?' exclaimed Squirrel, trying to see over their heads. 'Such a lot of people I never did see!'

Led by the Bens they made a circuit of the Lighthouse gallery but there was no sign of Baldmoney anywhere. Squirrel hopped up on the railing and peered over. Far below were black rocks on which a slow swell was swashing, gurgling and swilling among the fissures and clefts. The fog was lifting a little. If the unhappy Baldmoney had fallen into the sea, or upon those cruel crags, he could not have survived a moment.

Ben shook his head dolefully. 'I'm afraid he's gone, souls; we shan't see him again.'

But Squirrel was more cheerful. '*I* turned up all right after that night at Bantley Weir. Pan was watching over me then and he may be watching over Baldmoney. He may turn up safe and sound, he may have landed on the cliff behind us.'

They peered into the mist where the dim shape of a beetling hillside loomed not a hundred yards distant.

The wheeling rays of the Knockgobbin Light illuminated that desolate hill for a moment, before swinging round behind them. Yes, there *was* a chance he might be safe; at any rate, they made up their minds they would not give up hope.

Meanwhile, more and more birds seemed to be arriving. Warblers, martins, swallows, cuckoos, even such homely and familiar people as blackbirds and thrushes, came crowding on to the rails, or hovered stupidly in the full eye of the blazing beacon. It was a spectacle which the gnomes would never forget. So spellbound were they that they gave no thought of how they would ever leave the Knockgobbin Light, of how they would reach the mysterious country which lay so close to them.

By and by, the mist lifted magically; gleams and flashes of moonlit water revealed the uneasy sea. The smell of it was a new thing, the salty tang and clean scents of wrack, foreshore turf, and brackenny mountain filled their nostrils. With the lifting of the mist the multitudes crowding the rails and lighthouse top began to disperse their several ways. The night was full of many birds and whistling pinions. Curlews and plovers wailed, martins and swallows twittered, finches cheeped and Ben, suddenly feeling very full of himself, uttered a long drawn hoot. One by one the weary travellers took off once more; some heading for the open sea, others turning to the west, to the loom of the land.

And very soon—to the great surprise of the gnomes and Squirrel—they found they were alone with only the Bens and Lighthouse-mouse for company. Not a single bird remained!

Still the great light wheeled and swung, but its rays were paler now, for to the east the dawn was breaking and with it came a wind in little icy puffs. The dreadful night was nearly over.

Clear and distinct now against the rising sun there jutted a mighty cliff crowned with emerald turf and above the thin keening of gulls Dodder heard the voice of a lark. That tremulous song brought back a rush of homesickness; of other dawns, of Folly days, of the quiet pastures in river valleys, and the harvest fields beside Rumbling Mill.

Something scurried in the shadow of the lantern. It was Lighthouse-mouse. 'I shouldn't stay here if I were you, for it's Lighthouse Keeper who will be finding ye and there's no cover here.'

'But what are we to do?' cried Dodder, aghast to find their trials and tribulations were not yet over.

'I'll take you down,' said Ben. 'Climb on my back, it isn't far, and I'll come back for you, Sneezewort.'

'But what about Squirrel? He's *far* too heavy,' said Dodder. 'You could never take him on your back.'

'Quick, give me his parachute,' said Ben. 'I'll fold it up again and he can jump. There is turf below us on this side and it isn't far.'

They spread out Squirrel's parachute and Ben refolded

it cunningly and adjusted the harness round the body of the unfortunate animal.

'I've been nearly killed once,' he whimpered. 'I *can't* do it again!' It certainly seemed an awful drop, a very different matter too, in daylight.

But it was the only way, and the Bens and the gnomes half-carried the still-protesting Squirrel to the side, ignoring his squirms and squeaks. Frantically he clutched the rail and looked with horrified eyes at the cliff top underneath. But the next moment someone gave him a push and over he went.

The parachute opened and, with a sigh of relief, the gnomes saw their friend land safe and sound on the ground below.

After thanking Lighthouse-mouse for all his kindness, Sneezewort clambered up on the back of Mrs Ben and Dodder on to Mr Ben and before you could say 'Knife', all were standing on the short sweet turf.

How good it was to feel firm earth under them again!

Sneezewort seemed to go quite mad; he rolled about like a puppy, sniffing and clutching the grass. Squirrel, throwing away his parachute, skipped about like one demented, and Dodder soberly stumped up and down, blowing out his red cheeks and sniffing the keen morning air.

Over them towered the grey lighthouse, sharp against the dawn sky, and as Dodder glanced up at the rails so far above, he saw the light go out and the lantern cease to swing. A black figure with folded arms was standing there gazing seawards. It was the Lighthouse Keeper, stretching his legs. They had left not a moment too soon!

CHAPTER TWENTY-THREE

Woodcock's Island

hen Baldmoney jumped from the burning Wonderbird he was perhaps more frightened than anyone. He gave no thought to Squirrel and the others, all he knew was that he must get out somehow; in fact, I am afraid he lost his head.

For a split second he whizzed downwards. Then some invisible hand seemed to reach from above, hook a finger in his harness, and give a jerk to his falling body. His parachute had opened, and he, like the others, was drifting quietly to whatever horror lay below.

As he swung to and fro he heard the swish of water somewhere, that was all. Down, down, he floated towards the blazing light, just as Dodder and the others had done, but as he had been the first to jump he missed the top of the great

lantern by a matter of feet. The rails and blinding light
floated by, well out of reach, and the next moment he saw,
to his horror, that directly beneath was a pattern of white
foam and grey-green roller. Then he hit the water. As
Baldmoney weighed only a few ounces it was not a heavy
blow and the parachute helped to break it, but the shock
of the icy water took away his breath. He struggled
exactly like a bee which has fallen into a pond, and the
horrible salty stuff rushed into his mouth. He felt himself
dropping into the well of water, then up he swung at a
prodigious pace as, with a shattering roar, the great wave
hurled him far up the rocks, rolling him over and over
in a creamy smother of foam.

As luck would have it, as the roller sucked back for
another charge, he managed with his last strength to clutch
a limpet shell and there he clung, whimpering, his eyes
and nose full of salt water, and feeling half-stunned.

He had enough sense left to know that in another
moment the cruel sea would be on him again, so he
staggered to his feet and ran as fast as he could over the
slippery and weedy rocks. He had barely reached a patch
of sand between two massive boulders when he heard the
next roller coming. Shutting his eyes, he wedged himself
into a cranny and braced himself for the shock.

A wall of green water, laced with foam and bearing
on its crest tags of wet sea wrack, came curling over. The
terrified Baldmoney, screwing his head round, saw this
horrid mass of water suspended above him, then down it
came with an ear-splitting rumble and crash and in an
instant he was five feet under.

Shutting his eyes and clinging on for dear life, he
waited, holding his breath, and then came the terrible

drawing suck of the undertow which dragged at him like hungry claws.

Small pebbles and particles of sand were sucked back past him with a rattling sound. Again he was high and dry as though there was no water within miles. But Baldmoney was too wise to be deceived and getting to his feet once more he scurried over the rocks until he reached a band of rubbish, in which were broken bottles, twisted pieces of wood, old baskets, all the flotsam and jetsam of the sea's playground. Another roller crashed behind him but only the harmless foam reached him. It swilled about his knees in a rustling cream then sank into the bright pebbles.

Moving a few feet beyond the danger point the little gnome sat down, shivering. He had swallowed a lot of sea water and was violently sick. Then he felt better.

The mist was lifting. On his left reared the dark stack of the lighthouse, sending its rays over the desolate expanse of sea. The fret and roar of the angry waves filled his ears, his teeth were chattering like castanets, but he was held by an awful fascination of the wild and desolate scene.

And as he watched, with his knees drawn up under his beard and his hands clasped, he saw the mist draw off the ocean and the moonlight once again cast its eerie rays upon the dismal wastes of water.

The Knockgobbin Light sent out its long and brilliant fingers, blinding him as they turned in his direction. In the half darkness, white gulls flew by like ghosts, and to the east, behind the sombre shoulder of the hill, the sky was beginning to pale with the dawn.

Baldmoney knew not where he was, he had no idea

upon what desolate strand the Fates had cast him, whether his companions were alive or dead. He regarded himself as the only survivor and how he was going to make shift for himself was beyond his understanding.

He began to feel extremely hungry. What with his rude immersion and his cold and wet condition he felt he could sit down to a really good breakfast. So he at once began to cast along the foreshore to find something to eat.

It did not take him long to reach a rock covered with limpets. He knew they were shell-fish of some sort and he at once set to work. But all his efforts were fruitless. He hammered them with stones and tried to prise them off with his hunting knife, but it was all to no purpose. Very soon, however, salvation appeared in the shape of a large black bird with a grey hood. It was very like Kackjack, only larger, and it came hunting down the tideline towards Baldmoney. Now and again it alighted upon the wet sand and bore aloft a shell, which it let drop, to shatter the hard mussel upon the rocks. Down dived the bird again and made his feast. It seemed to Baldmoney a good way of getting one's breakfast, so without more ado he hurried along the sand, picking his way over snake-like coils of glistening seaweed and bladder-wrack, until he came up with the strange bird.

Baldmoney, who always believed in being polite to foreigners, took off his skin cap which (strange to say) had survived his battle with the sea, and made the crow a polite bow.

'Is it a gnome that I see?' asked the astonished crow, stopping in the middle of gulping down a large piece of mussel.

'My name is Baldmoney,' said our hero, 'and I am, I

believe, the sole survivor of an accident which happened in the night and in which, through Pan's Providence, I have escaped with my life. You see before you a poor hungry castaway, not knowing to what country the fates have brought him, nor what further tribulations may befall him.'

'Och! but I'm sorry for ye,' said the crow, who was obviously a 'local', 'but as to your being hungry, why it's me that will find you something to eat. My name is Hoddie. I, like you, have little in the world, save a suit of feathers and perhaps a better notion than most people how to look after myself. As to where ye are, it's strange ye should not be knowing that. Yonder is the Knockgobbin Light and this soil on which ye stand is Ireland, the best country in the whole wide world. And it's you I'll be congratulatin' for your deliverance. Was it a ship that was wrecked?'

'No, Mr Hoddie, 'twas not a ship but a Wonderbird which the Bens—they are owls, you know—and myself built, away in England.'

'Oh, so it's England, is it, that you've come from? I should have known it now I come to think a little, for I know by your manner of speaking you are no Irish gnome.'

'Then this *is* Woodcock's island?' said Baldmoney. 'It's the very place we were making for when the fog came down. I think Ben lost his way—Ben was towing us you see—and then Dodder's pipe set fire to the plane—he *would* smoke, of course—and a spark from it set us all ablaze and we had to jump for our lives. Our friend Squirrel, who was making the journey with us, and my two brothers, Dodder and Sneezewort; I fear they have been drowned and I shall never see them again!'

'It's hard on you, all alone in a strange country with no kith nor kin to comfort ye. But let it never be said we lack hospitality in this island. First ye shall have something to be putting inside of ye. D'you like mussel, fresh mussel?'

'I've never tasted sea mussels,' said Baldmoney truthfully, 'only freshwater ones. We find them, you know, in our streams and ponds at home, and sometimes we find pearls in them.'

'Oh, to be shure yes, *I* find pearls now and then and give them to the Leprechauns way back in the Mourne mountains. But I'll get busy and it's a fine breakfast I'll be getting you if you will but sit on the rock there and have a little patience!'

So Baldmoney sat on the rock indicated by Hoddie while the good-natured bird went beating down the tide.

A blaze of silver and gold showed in the east, the whole rugged coast was now clearly visible, the jutting tongue of land on which stood the Knockgobbin Light, the jagged rocks beneath, and the white rollers fretting on the shore, all were now distinct; landwards rose a line of blue hills higher than any Baldmoney had ever seen.

Now the new day was born the white gulls came streaming from the cliffs and far out, off Knockgobbin Light, a gannet was diving into the surf getting his breakfast.

What a night it had been, thought Baldmoney; what a terrible dream the whole thing seemed and, despite Hoddie's kindness, what would he do all alone in a strange land?

He had heard before that there were still Little People in Woodcock's island, indeed from what Hoddie had let drop about giving the pearls to the Leprechauns this fact was now confirmed, but he knew not what manner of

Folk they were. They might prove hostile to him and he wasn't sure that Leprechauns were gnomes at all. They might be elves or pixies who are mischievous, quarrelsome little creatures, who are only half as intelligent as a gnome.

All he wanted was to see the familiar and dear faces of his own kith and kin and he felt he could face any trials or dangers which might be forthcoming.

But though he hopefully scanned the cliffs and shore he saw no sign of any survivors from the wreck. His fervent prayer was that the Bens would be somewhere near. They at any rate would be safe unless, dazzled by the great lantern, they had broken their necks, as many another feathered traveller had done. But he looked in vain for the familiar shapes of the owls; only multitudes of white gulls weaved in front of the towering stacks.

Before long he spied his saviour returning. The crow circled overhead, hovered like a kestrel and a fat mussel shell came whizzing down—smack!—on the rock beside him. Eagerly picking out the shell fragments from the juicy orange fish, which appeared not unlike a nicely poached egg, he set about his meal with pardonable gusto.

The Folly mussels had been nice and so had those they found on Poplar Island, but this mussel! . . . no words of mine can convey how delicious it was and how it tickled Baldmoney's palate. He was famished and he ate and ate and barely had he finished one when smash!—another lay beside him—until he could eat no more.

He wiped his mouth on a piece of seaweed and fumbled for his pipe. Though not such an inveterate smoker as Dodder, Baldmoney enjoyed his after-breakfast 'draw' and he was disgusted to find his tobacco—made out of dried, wild mint leaves—was a sodden mess. So he laid it out on top of the rock to dry. The scent of it made him very homesick, for that mint had been gathered at Rumbling Mill.

Hoddie was very attentive. Having fed his guest he came and perched on a rock close by and preened himself and hunted for fleas. Baldmoney, feeling he must make some return, offered to help. It was a service he had frequently done for the Bens and his other bird friends. The fleas were nasty grey flat creatures which sidled between the feathers, but Baldmoney was as sharp as a monkey and very soon Hoddie had not one left.

I may be taken to task for mentioning this performance but pests such as ticks and lice are a constant source of worry to all kinds of birds and wild animals and Baldmoney thought no more of the business than you and I do of cleaning our teeth.

By the time Baldmoney had finished, his tobacco was dry and filling his favourite pipe (cut from a hazel up the Folly Brook), he found some dead grass, twisted it up into a spill and lit it by means of his flints which he always carried in an inner pocket. Hoddie was very interested, for he had never before seen a gnome smoke and such a practice was unknown among the Leprechauns.

'Now, what's to do?' asked Baldmoney, when he had got his pipe well alight. The sun had warmed him and dried his skin clothes and he felt particularly 'beany' and full of vigour. It was partly due to realization of his miraculous escape. No doubt Pan had engineered it and if so the Bens and the other gnomes were probably safe too. At least he sincerely hoped so.

Hoddie, sitting in the sun, and no longer irritated by his unwelcome guests, also felt pleased with life in general. 'If I were you,' said he, 'I shouldn't be leaving this place just yet. Your pals may turn up and I'm thinking of an excellent temporary home for you and not very far away to be sure.'

'Indeed, and where is that, pray?'

'It's an old wreck I'm thinking of, just round the next cliff. It's well up on the rocks and the highest tide won't reach it, not enough to cause you any inconvenience. She's the *Rose Marie*, a crab boat, which came ashore six years ago; she stove her bottom in on the rocks. That's the place where ye'll be as snug as snug.'

The suggestion sounded quite good to Baldmoney and so crow and gnome walked along the shore until, on passing a mass of rock, he saw the remains of the ship lying among some weedy slabs not thirty yards away. Four shags were perched on her battered bow drying their wings. They held them out wide apart, now and again giving them a little shake.

Now there is something very fascinating about an old wreck, and Baldmoney, who still loved ships, was entranced with her. Her mighty timbers were draped in seaweed and there was an exciting smell of sea water, weed and fish about her, and she was crusted with limpets and barnacles.

Most of the hulk had been smashed and broken by the waves, but the fo'castle remained almost intact and no better place could be imagined in which to make a temporary home. There was shelter and it would not be difficult to find firing. Enough wood lay about to keep him in fuel indefinitely.

Baldmoney could see that Hoddie was anxious to be off, for he had a call to pay on a jackdaw along the cliffs to discuss some matter or other, and after promising to be back before sundown, the crow flew away and Baldmoney was left alone. Now the stress and strain was over, he felt very tired. The sun was strong and anyway gnomes dislike bright daylight. So he crawled into a corner of the old fo'castle and finding a comfortable bed of dried seaweed he lay down for a nap. The sleepy wash of waves and the still more lulling cries of gulls soon sent him into a deep slumber.

It was strange to think that only twenty-four hours before he and the others were up Sperrywell Lane, so many leagues across the sea. So much can happen in a little time!

It was a peaceful spot: the weed-strewn wreck, its curved timbers and rotting decks glistening in the bright sunshine; the white receding foam sliding and returning up the sand; the wheeling gulls dipping and flashing against the blue sky; the vivid green of the cliff-top turf—all made up a perfect picture.

Within the old fo'castle the sounds of breakers, gulls, and wind seemed to echo strangely. What junk lay about in the bowels of the wreck! Rusty chains, each link heavier by many times than Baldmoney, a huge anchor, encrusted with barnacles, the remains of old spars and cordage, oyster and mussel shells dropped by birds, the carcass of a herring gull almost as big as a goose, its juices dried so that it smelt only of the sea and bleached bone; bottles; three old crab pots which had not held a prisoner within their bars these many years; bent nails and masses of bladder-wrack cast there and now dried and glittering with salt: all these things had one smell as a common denominator—the smell of the sea.

The shadow from the old crab boat sidled round on the sand, the tide began to turn again and advance over the rocks as it had done for—oh! I don't know how many times.

It crept on until at last it touched the rotten beam of the old crab boat at the stern. Hoddie had been right about high water. The fo'castle was never covered, even by the highest tide. When on that fearful night of storm and wind six years before, the sea had struggled to crush and drown the *Rose Marie*, the very wind which had striven to encompass its destruction had hurled her far up upon the rocks out of the reach of further torture. So Baldmoney was as secure as if he were leagues inland by the Folly Brook.

The beards of seaweed which grew on the stern timbers and which were wetted twice daily by the tides, began to float out flat, rejoicing in the coming of their life's blood, and crabs came, sidling between the crannies and crevices of the old hulk. Numberless little fish came a-visiting, peering with fixed expression into the weed tangles, and weary jellyfish sought refuge for a brief half hour ere the tide should drop once more.

Baldmoney slept on and as he slept he dreamt a dream. It was springtime on the Folly Brook and the catkins were hanging over the stream, but for all the joy of awakening life he was tortured by a dreadful fear. He must hurry, hurry, hurry, for they had lost the key of the *Jeanie Deans* and could not wind up the engine. Away over Moss Mill a terrible storm was gathering, the sky inky black and slashed with vivid forks of lightning.

But Dodder had lost the key and not all their efforts

could reveal its hiding place and all the while those menacing clouds were drawing ever nearer.

And then Dodder found it in one of his old jacket pockets and everyone tumbled aboard, Squirrel too, and the Bens. Off they went down the river but the storm kept gaining on them until the sky grew so dark Dodder had to light the cabin lamp. Those fearful shafts of zizzling light whipped up the waters; waves began to break over the boat. The *Jeanie Deans* was filling, filling, until at last, with a lurch, she sank and Baldmoney seemed to be falling through miles of space . . . He opened his eyes, and there he was, in the weedy timbers of the old crab boat and not a foot away stood a group of people, familiar people. At first, Baldmoney thought he was still dreaming. There was Dodder, grinning from ear to ear, Squirrel fluffing his tail, and Sneezewort hopping about on one leg; there were the Bens, perched on the side of the boat, peering down at him and blinking, and there was . . . who do you think? . . . why, Woodcock, dear old Woodcock, with his high, wise head and friendly eye!

Dodder stumped forward, walking carefully because the seaweed was so slippery. 'Wake up, Baldmoney, wake up, old fellow, thanks to you we've made the trip and everyone's safe and sound!'

'Safe and sound!' muttered Baldmoney rubbing his eyes. 'Oh dear, am I still dreaming? Come here, Dodder and let me hug you, Sneezewort too, Woodcock, Squirrel, and the Bens! I thought I should never see you again!'

'We've got Woodcock to thank for that,' said Dodder, clapping his hand on the worthy bird's shoulder. 'Hoddie told him he'd met a gnome on the beach and he sent us all along here and, what's more, Baldmoney my boy,

Woodcock's island, his own *special* island he told us about, is only an hour's march over the hills, we'll be there before sun-up tomorrow!'

Baldmoney could not speak, his heart was too full. He sat looking first at Dodder and then at the others and he felt unutterably thankful. In his ears was the low wash of the waves and high overhead a star was winking. And as they all stood there in the shadows of the old crab boat, each one of them heard another sound above the voice of the sea. It was a sound which they had heard before, a long, long time ago, that same music which floated out in the moonlit glades of Crow Wood, the same which Otter had heard at Bantley Weir.

Off came their caps, Woodcock inclined his bill, and the Bens bowed down until their big spotted foreheads touched the timbers of the boat. Can you guess what that sound was? Of course you can! It was the Pipes of Pan!

There is a green little island set in a grey, grey loch in the very heart of the blue hills. On the island is a ruined chapel where an old saint lies sleeping, the wild geese take their rest there and the rabbits play. Hard by is a wood of bog oak where Squirrel takes his pleasure and in the ivied ruin the Bens have reared several families of woolly owlets, each with an Irish accent, but that is not to be wondered at. No mortal disturbs the Little Grey Men save in the fishing season when anglers sometimes land to eat their midday sandwiches under the crumbling walls of the hermit's cell. But the boatmen do not like going there, they say the place is haunted, and that sometimes, on wild autumn and winter nights, a tiny light is seen winking in and out among the chapel stones. But you and I are wiser.

We know that the light is from the gnomes' fire as they grill their supper of troutlings.

And now I suppose you will be asking, will the Little Grey Men ever come back?

All I can say to that is that the Stream People have not forgotten them and not a spring passes but every moorhen chick, every new vole baby, every otter cub, is told by its parents of the Little Grey Men, of how they lived long ago on the Folly banks and sailed away in the *Jeanie Deans*, and how, one day, they will see them again.

As for me, great lumbering mortal that I am, I believe that too, and every spring when I see the catkins breaking I keep my eyes and ears open. And if you take my advice, you will also. After all, the Stream People must know what they are talking about!

By the same author

The Little Grey Men

Winner of the Carnegie Medal

The last gnomes in Britain live by a Warwickshire brook. their names are Dodder, Baldmoney, Cloudberry, and Sneezewort, and their home is under an oak tree which grows on the banks of the Folly.

Cloudberry decides to go and explore—he wants to find out what lies beyond the Folly. But when he doesn't return, it is up to his three remaining brothers to build a boat and set out to find him.

This is the story of the brothers' epic journey in search of Cloudberry and is set against the background of the English countryside, beginning in spring, continuing through summer, and concluding in autumn, when the first frosts are starting to arrive.

Other Oxford Books

Tom's Midnight Garden
Philippa Pearce

Winner of the Carnegie Medal

Tom has to spend the summer at his aunt's and it seems as if nothing good will ever happen again. Then he hears the grandfather clock strike thirteen—and everything changes. Outside the door is a garden—a garden that shouldn't exist. Are the children there ghosts—or is it Tom who is the ghost?

Minnow on the Say
Philippa Pearce

David couldn't believe his eyes. Wedged by the landing stage at the bottom of the garden was a canoe. The *Minnow*. David traces the canoe's owner, Adam, and they begin a summer of adventures. The *Minnow* takes them on a treasure hunt along the river. But they are not the only people looking for treasure, and soon they are caught in a race against time . . .

The Little Bookroom
Eleanor Farjeon

A girl sits in a dusty room, crammed to the rafters with books. Sunlight dances on the covers, between which are stories of magical worlds and faraway places, lands of princesses, kings, giants, and real children too.

Eleanor Farjeon was that girl, who was so enchanted by her little bookroom that she recreated it by writing this wonderful collection of short stories.

This charming book was the winner of the prestigious Carnegie Medal and is beautifully illustrated throughout by Edward Ardizzone, whose exquisite pictures immediately bring to mind the magical atmosphere of the stories.

The Ship That Flew
Hilda Lewis

Peter sees the model ship in the shop window and he wants it more than anything else on earth. But it is no ordinary model. The ship takes Peter and his brother and sisters on magical flights, wherever they ask to go. They fly around the world and back into the past. But how long can you keep a ship that is worth everything in the world, and a bit over...?

A Little Lower than the Angels
Geraldine McCaughrean

Winner of the Whitbread Children's Novel Award

Gabriel has no idea what the future will hold when he runs away from his apprenticeship with the bad-tempered stonemason. But God Himself, in the shape of playmaster Garvey, has plans for him. He wants Gabriel for his angel . . . But will Gabriel's new life with the travelling players be any more secure? In a world of illusion, people are not always what they seem. Least of all Gabriel.

The Great Elephant Chase
Gillian Cross

Winner of The Smarties Prize and the Whitbread Children's Novel Award

The elephant changed their lives for ever. Because of the elephant, Tad and Cissie become entangled in a chase across America, by train, by flatboat and steam boat. Close behind is Hannibal Jackson, who is determined to have the elephant for himself. And how do you hide an enormous Indian elephant?